STELLA MARIS

STELLA MARIS

Cormac McCarthy

ALFRED A. KNOPF New York

2022

THIS IS A BORZOI BOOK
PUBLISHED BY ALFRED A. KNOPF

Copyright © 2022 by M-71, Ltd.

All rights reserved. Published in the United States by Alfred A. Knopf,
a division of Penguin Random House LLC, New York, and distributed
in Canada by Penguin Random House Canada Limited, Toronto.

www.aaknopf.com

Knopf, Borzoi Books, and the colophon are
registered trademarks of Penguin Random House LLC.

ISBN 9780307269003 (hardcover)
ISBN 9780593535233 (ebook)
ISBN 9781524712402 (open market)

Library of Congress Control Number: 2022934755

Front-of-jacket images: (left) James Thew/Alamy;
(right) Victority/Alamy
Spine- and back-of-jacket image: James Thew/Alamy
Jacket design by Chip Kidd

Manufactured in Canada
First Edition

STELLA MARIS

STELLA MARIS

Black River Falls, Wisconsin

Established 1902

Since 1950 a non-denominational facility and hospice
for the care of psychiatric medical patients.

Resident Unit   October 27, 1972
Case 72-118

Patient is a twenty-year-old Jewish/Caucasian
female. Attractive, possibly anorexic. Arrived
at this facility six days ago apparently by bus
and without luggage. Admission signed by Dr
Wegner. Patient had a plastic bag full of hundred
dollar bills in her purse—something over forty
thousand dollars—which she attempted to give to
the receptionist. Patient is a doctoral candidate
in mathematics at the University of Chicago and
has been diagnosed as paranoid schizophrenic with
a longstanding aetiology of visual and auditory
hallucinations. Resident of this facility on two
prior occasions.

I

Hi. I'm Dr Cohen.

You're not the Dr Cohen I was expecting.

Sorry about that. That would be Dr Robert Cohen.

Yes. I guess there's no shortage of Dr Cohens.

Probably not. How are you? Are you all right?

Am I all right.

Yes.

I'm in the looney bin.

Well. Other than that, I suppose.

How long have you been doing this?

About fourteen years.

You're going to record this.

I think that was the agreement. Is that all right?

I suppose. At the time I thought you were somebody else.

It's not all right.

No. It's okay. Although I should say that I only agreed to chat. Not to any kind of therapy.

Yes. Is there anything you'd like to ask me? Before we begin.

We have begun. Such as what?

Maybe you should tell me a little about yourself.

Oh boy.

No?

Are we going to paint by the numbers?

I'm sorry?

It's all right. It's just that I'm naive enough to keep imagining that it's possible to launch these sorties on a vector not wrenched totally implausible by cant.

It's what? My tone of voice?

It's all right. We'll do it your way. What the hell.

Well. I dont want to get off to a bad start. I just thought you might want to tell me a little about why you're here.

I didnt have anyplace else to go.

And why here.

I'd been here before.

Why originally, then.

Because I couldnt get into Coletta.

And why Coletta?

It was where they sent Rosemary Kennedy. After her father had her brains scooped out.

Do you have some connection with the family?

No. I didnt know anything about psychiatric centers. I just figured that if that was the place they'd come up with it was probably a pretty good place. I think they scooped her brains out someplace else, actually.

You're talking about a lobotomy.

Yes.

Why did they do that to her?

Because she was weird and her father was afraid someone was going to fuck her. She wasnt what the old man had in mind.

Is that true?

Yes. Unfortunately.

Why did you feel you had to go someplace?

You mean this time?

Yes. This time.

I just did. I'd left Italy. Where my brother was in a coma. They kept trying to get my permission to pull the plug. To sign the papers. So I fled. I didnt know what else to do.

It was something you couldnt bring yourself to do? Take him off life support?

Yes.

Is he brain-dead?

I dont want to talk about my brother.

All right. Just tell me why he's in a coma.

He was in a car wreck. He was a racecar driver. I really dont.

All right. Is there anything you'd like to ask me?

About what?

Anything. About me if you like. May I call you Alicia?

You want me to ask you about yourself.

If you like. Yes.

You teach at the University.

At Madison. Yes.

I know where the University is. You dress rather well for an academician.

Thank you.

It wasnt a compliment. You're not a psychoanalyst.

I'm a psychiatrist.

You're not an MD.

I am. In fact.

What else.

I'm married. I have two children. My wife runs a children's program for the city. I'm forty-three years old.

What do you get up to when no one's looking?

I dont. And you?

I smoke an occasional cigarette. I dont drink or use drugs. Or take medication. You dont have any cigarettes I dont suppose.

No. I could bring some.

Okay.

What else?

I have clandestine conversations with supposedly nonexistent personages. I've been called a you-know-what teaser but I dont think that's true. People seem to find me interesting but I've pretty much given up talking to them. I talk to my fellow loonies.

You dont talk to other mathematicians?

Not anymore. Well. Some.

Why is that?

It's a long story.

Are you still working at mathematics?

No. Not what you'd call mathematics.

What sort of mathematics were you doing?

Topology. Topos theory.

But you're not doing that anymore.

No. I got distracted.

What was it that distracted you?

Topology. Topos theory.

Maybe we should skip the mathematics for the time being.

That's fine. I didnt know what I was doing anyway.

I'm surprised to hear you say that. Couldnt you get help from some of the other mathematicians?

No. They didnt know either.

You're sure it's all right about the recording?

Sure. What if I say fuck or something? I think I did, actually. Actually there it is again.

I dont know. I think the agreement was that you wouldnt have any editing privileges.

I'm not really serious.

Oh.

Alicia's okay. I prefer it to Henrietta.

You're not being serious again.

No.

All right. You dont want to tell me anything about your brother?

This is starting to sound like the Eliza Program. No. I dont. Want to.

The computer psychiatric program.

Yes.

All right. What would you like to talk about?

I dont know. I think I just want to be a smartass. If you want to actually talk to me we're going to have to cut through at least some of the bullshit. Dont you think? Or do you?

I do. I think you're absolutely right.

Such as that.

Is that bullshit?

Of course it's bullshit. No way in hell do you think I'm absolutely right.

I see.

And please dont say I see.

It just means I'm trying to understand your point of view. Is there anyone you're in contact with?

You mean real people?

Preferably. Yes.

Not really.

No mathematicians? No one from the University?

I thought we werent going to talk about mathematics.

All right.

I still write to Grothendieck but he's left IHES and he doesnt write back. Which is all right. I dont expect him to.

Is he a mathematician?

Yes. Or he was.

Where does he live?

I dont know where he lives. I suppose he's still in France.

It's not a very French name.

It's not a French name at all. His father's name was Schapiro.

Later Tanaroff. He has no citizenship. He was a displaced child in the war. Hiding. Running for his life. His father died at Auschwitz.

Where do you send the letters?

To IHES. You dont know who he is, do you?

No.

It's all right. We were friends. We are friends. We share a common skepticism.

About what?

About mathematics.

I'm not sure that I follow you.

It's all right.

You're skeptical about mathematics?

Yes.

You feel disappointed in the discipline in some way? I'm not sure how you can be skeptical about the entire subject.

I know.

But it has disappointed you.

That would be one way to put it.

How would it do that?

Well. In this case it was led by a group of evil and aberrant and wholly malicious partial differential equations who had conspired to usurp their own reality from the questionable circuitry of its creator's brain not unlike the rebellion which Milton describes and to fly their colors as an independent nation unaccountable to God or man alike. Something like that.

You think my questions are naive.

I'm sorry. No. I dont. The failure doesnt lie with the querent.

Is he a prominent mathematician? Your friend.

Grothendieck. He's widely regarded as the foremost mathematician of the twentieth century. If you ignore the fact that Hilbert and Poincaré and Dedekind and Cantor all lived into the twentieth century. Which you should, since all their major work was done in the nineteenth. And I'm not all that big a fan of von Neumann.

I'm sorry but I dont know those names.

I know. It's all right. Well, not really. But it's okay.

Grothendieck.

Yes.

Did you work with him?

I dont know if you would call it work. We spent a lot of time talking. He would come to the Institute on Tuesdays. And I spent a lot of time at his house. I would eat with the family. Then the conversations would go on into the night. In a sense we were just in the same nuthouse together. The Institute had been established for him and another mathematician named Dieudonné by a wealthy Russian named Motchane—if that in fact was his real name—who was mad as a hatter. It was modeled after the IAS. At Princeton. Oppenheimer was an advisor. I was there for a year, but at that time the funds had begun to dry up. In the end I never got all of my fellowship money. I was the only woman there. At first they thought I worked in the kitchen.

I take it it was not a good experience.

It was fantastic. Even at Chicago I'd had a certain amount of trouble. But Grothendieck would listen to every word you said. Nodding and scribbling on his pad. Talking. Asking you questions you hadnt asked yourself.

How old were you?

Seventeen.

And that wasnt an issue. Your age.

It wouldnt even occur to him.

Why doesnt he write?

Mostly because he's given up mathematics.

As have you.

Yes. As have I.

Was that hard?

Well. I think maybe it's harder to lose just one thing than to lose everything.

One thing could be everything.

Yes. It could. Mathematics was all we had. It's not like we gave up mathematics and took up golf. Now he gets invited to seminars to talk and he shows up and rants about the environment or the warmongers. His parents were political activists. He's very devoted to their memory. He has a pencil drawing of his father on his desk and what I'm told is a deathmask of his mother. But the truth is that they abandoned him as a child to pursue their political dream of a world that will never be and my guess is that he felt compelled to take up their cause in order to justify their betrayal of him. He's married and has children. And I'm afraid that he'll do the same thing.

Are you crying?

I'm sorry.

But he gave it all up.

Yes.

Why?

His friends believe that he has become increasingly unstable mentally.

Has he?

It's complicated. You end up talking about belief. About the nature of reality. Anyway, some of my fellow mathematicians would be entertained to hear abandoning mathematics presented as evidence of mental instability.

How old is he?

He's forty-four.

And you went to France to accept a fellowship at his Institute.

I went to France to be with my brother. I didnt know if he was coming back. But yes. I wanted to go to the Institute. They were doing what I wanted to do.

You'd already graduated from the University of Chicago.

Yes.

At sixteen.

Yes. I was in the doctoral program. I still am, I suppose. I had no life, really. All I did was work.

If you had not become a mathematician what would you like to have been?

Dead.

How serious a response is that?

I took your question seriously. You should take my response seriously.

Are you okay?

Yes. Maybe I did sort of blow off your question. What I really wanted was a child. What I do really want. If I had a child I would just go in at night and sit there. Quietly. I would listen to my child breathing. If I had a child I wouldnt care about reality.

You surprise me.

Yes. Well.

Do you want to go on?

I'm all right. In any event Grothendieck and Motchane had a falling-out. Motchane told him that the Institute was accepting military money so that he would resign. Which he did. I'm not even sure if it was true. About the money.

Is he really a great mathematician?

Yes.

Is there anything he did that I might understand?

I dont know. He's turned out more work than any five mathematicians should be expected to. Approaching Euler. Finally he set out to rewrite all of algebraic geometry. He only got through about a third of it. Several thousand pages. But he changed mathematics fundamentally. He led the Bourbaki group but in the end they couldnt follow him. Or wouldnt. Their mathematics was grounded in set theory—which was beginning to look more and more porous—and he'd moved a good bit beyond that. To a whole new level of logical abstraction. A new way of looking at the world. He was completing what Riemann started. To unseat Euclid forever. Ignoring for now the Fifth Postulate. The intrusion of infinity which Euclid couldnt deal with. When you get to topos theory you are at the edge of another universe. You have found a place to stand where you can look back at the world from nowhere. It's not just some gestalt. It's fundamental.

You committed yourself here.

At Stella Maris.

Yes.

If you get committed you get certified but if you commit yourself you dont. They figure that you must be reasonably sane or you wouldnt have shown up. On your own. So you get a pass as far as the records are concerned. If you're sane enough to know that you're crazy then you're not as crazy as if you thought you were sane.

You've been here what? Twice before?

Yes.

Why this time? I guess is what I'm asking.

I kept encountering strange people in my room.

Apparently that's nothing new.

I wanted to see some people here.

Patients.

Yes. You think I'd come here to visit with the help?

You mean the counselors.

Yes.

I dont know.

Sure you do.

You're not on any medication.

No.

Do you think that's wise?

I dont know what's wise. I'm not a wise person.

But you dont think you're crazy.

I dont know. No. At least I dont fit in your crazy book.

The DSM.

Yes. Of course I'm not the only one who's not in there.

Are you still having hallucinations?

I never said that they were hallucinations.

You referred to your visitors as nonexistent persons.

Personages.

Personages then.

I was quoting from the literature.

What literature is that?

The literature on me. But no. I havent seen them lately. They dont like to come around a place like this. It makes them uncomfortable. You're smiling.

You seem almost to be saying that such a facility in itself promotes mental health. What? In the manner of a church fending off evil spirits?

I suppose that could be an okay analogy. The Church never tires of talking about sinners. The saved hardly get a mention. Someone pointed out that Satan's interests are wholly spiritual. Chesterton, I think.

I'm not sure I understand.

Satan is only interested in your soul. He doesnt give a shit about your welfare otherwise.

Interesting. Your visitors. Whatever they are. What can you tell me about them?

I never know how to answer that question. What is it that you want to know?

Do they come with names?

Nobody comes with names. You give them names so that you can find them in the dark. I know you've read my file but the good doctors pay scant attention to any descriptions of hallucinatory figures.

How real do they seem to you? They have what? A dreamlike quality?

I dont think so. Dream figures lack coherence. You see bits and pieces and you fill in the rest. Sort of like your ocular blindspot. They lack continuity. They morph into other beings. Not to mention that the landscape they occupy is a dream landscape.

The principal figure is a bald dwarf.

A small person. Yes.

The Kid.

The Kid. Yes.

But he's not like a figure in your dreams.

No. He's like a figure in your room.

I wonder if you have any opinion as to why these figures should take on the particular appearance which they do.

Would you like to try another question? They take on the appearance of which their appearance is composed. I suppose what you really want to know is what they might be symbolic of. I've no idea. I'm not a Jungian. Your question suggests too that you think there might be some possibility of orchestrating this inane menagerie. Somehow or other. Each figure of which all but shimmers with reality. I can see the hairs in their nostrils and I can see into their earholes and I can see the knots in their shoelaces. You think that you might be able to stage out of this an opera of my troubled mental processes. I wish you luck.

But you're aware that other people dont believe that beings such as these exist.

Define exist.

Sorry?

I'm not really concerned with what other people believe. I dont consider them qualified to have an opinion.

Because they havent seen them.

Well. I think that qualifies as a logical dead end. What do you think?

I'm sure you know that hallucinations on the scale at which you describe yours are vanishingly rare. More than one counselor has suggested that you were making them up.

Making them up.

Yes.

That comes off as a rather odd locution, doesnt it?

That you were making it up that you were making them up.

Yes, well. They're not entitled to an opinion either.

The counselors?

The counselors.

Maybe not. When did this business start? At what age?

Do you think that I present as a florid psychotic?

No. I dont. But then of course you dont like to be tested.

No. Do you?

No. Unless I think I'm going to do well. But you think that tests in general are what? Misguided? Invasive?

Let's just say that I dont like them.

But you took some of the tests. You made a perfect score on the advanced Raven's.

It's been done before.

Not in the time in which you did it.

The initial questions are pretty stupid. You just fill in the figure that's missing. It's only compound in a fairly primitive way. The problems get more difficult but they're not really different. Besides, no matter how complex the figures become there are still no more than six rules.

At the end of the test you sketched in a couple of three-dimensional matrices.

Lattices. Yes. One of them was geometric and the other was computational. They werent that difficult. But I thought they looked promising. I saw that they could get pretty gnarly pretty quickly. If you didnt get the dimensionality right you couldnt follow the progression. I never heard back from them. But it was my sense that if people could ace the tests you'd come up with then you probably needed tougher tests. I thought you wanted to talk about the horts?

About the what?

The horts. The entities. Horts as in cohorts.

Is that a word? Horts?

It is now. I suppose the closest word to it would be orts. In English a piece, in German a place. Anyway, at what age. To your question. At the onset of menses I think it says in the file.

I just wondered if that was correct. That's rather early.

You could even call it precocious.

I hope you'll excuse the question but at what age was this?

Twelve.

Schizophrenia typically doesnt occur in females until the late teens or early twenties.

I've never been legitimately diagnosed as schizophrenic.

No.

Maybe they'll devise a test for general weirdness. Whatcha think?

You took the MMPI here. Two years ago.

All right.

Speaking of general weirdness. You were classified as a sociopathic deviant followed by a number of other rather unattractive adjectives. This was on scale four. Did you know the Minnesota test?

No. I dont sit around studying your tests. I find them breathtakingly stupid and meaningless. So I just kept getting more and more pissed off. In the end I was trying to qualify as a possibly homicidal lunatic.

You werent concerned about being confined?

I was confined.

You didnt find anything interesting about the Minnesota test.

No.

You scored ninety-six on the Stanford-Binet.

I was trying to score a hundred.

Why?

Because that's what you're supposed to score.

What is your actual IQ?

I dont have one.

This is not a form of hubris? Being untestable?

Not if you're not. Anyway, the Stanford-Binet is racist. Among other things.

How can it be racist?

There are no questions about music on the test. For instance. Apparently music doesnt count. So here's a black guy with a measured IQ of eighty-five who is by any metric you might care to choose a musical genius. Simply off the charts. But to the IQ folks he's little more than a halfwit.

I suppose you think the test-people themselves are not all that bright.

I've never met anyone in this business who had any grasp at all of mathematics. And intelligence is numbers. It's not words. Words are things we've made up. Mathematics is not. The math and logic questions on the IQ tests are a joke.

How did it get that way? Intelligence as numerical.

Maybe it always was. Or maybe we actually got there by counting. For a million years before the first word was ever said. If you want an IQ of over a hundred and fifty you'd better be good with numbers.

I would think it would be difficult for someone to assemble the responses which you did on some of these tests without being familiar with the test.

I'd had a certain amount of practice. I had to make A's in the humanities in college without reading the idiotic material assigned.

You wouldnt read the material on principle?

No. I just didnt have time.

Why didnt you have time?

Because I was doing math eighteen hours a day.

Some people would say that's not possible.

Yes. They would.

What about scale eight?

I dont know what that is.

Well, among other things it's designed to test for schizophrenia.

Yeah? How'd I do?

You squeaked past. So if you were manipulating the test might it not mean you were schizoid and somehow managed to lie about it? Of course the test is also designed to pick up head trauma and epilepsy.

I was dropped on my head as a child.

Is that true?

No.

All this math you were doing. It cant have all been assigned material.

None of it was assigned material.

What was it that interested you most?

I spent a certain amount of time on game theory. There's something seductive about it. Von Neumann got caught up in it. Maybe that's not the right term. But I think I finally began to see that it promised explanations it wasnt capable of supplying. It really is game theory. It's not something else. Conway or no Conway. Everything that you start out with is a tool, but your hope is that it actually comprises a theory.

But game theory is a theory isnt it?

If you say so.

You were living in the attic at your grandmother's house.

Yes. After my mother died. Bobby fixed it up for me.

And this is where the apparitions first appeared?

Yes.

What were they doing while you were doing all this math?

I dont know. After a while I pretty much ignored them. Except for the Kid. He was pretty hard to ignore.

I'm puzzled that you didnt find them more disturbing.

Well. I was twelve. How would I know that it wasnt normal?

But you did know.

I knew that it wasnt normal. But I didnt know that it wasnt normal for me.

Why is he called the Kid?

It's short for the Thalidomide Kid. He doesnt have any hands. Just these flippers.

This is the dwarf.

Small person.

Who else?

Just a lot of characters. Entertainers. Supposedly.

Did you find them entertaining?

No.

And they just appear. Out of nowhere.

As opposed to what? Out of somewhere? All right. Nowhere. We'll stick with nowhere. Look. I know this conversation pretty much by heart.

From other counselors.

Yes.

What would you like me to do?

Surprise me.

Surprise you.

Yes. Well. I wont hold my breath. The factual and the suspect are both subject to the same dimming with time. There is a fusion in the memory of events which is at loose ends where reality is concerned. You wake from a nightmare with a certain relief. But that doesnt erase it. It's always there. Even after it's forgotten. The haunting sense that there is something you have not understood will remain long after. What you were trying to ask me. The answer is no. They simply arrive. Unannounced. No strange odors, no music. I listen to them. Sometimes. Sometimes I just go to sleep.

Can you sleep with them in the room?

This is like having a conversation with Zeno. Have you thought about that question? Isnt it funny how it's always in the last place you look.

All right. But in general you dont find them frightening.

No.

And that doesnt seem strange to you.

No. I was twelve. I probably thought they accompanied puberty. Everybody else did. Anyway, it was the puberty that was frightening, not the phantoms. The more naive your life the more frightening your dreams. Your unconscious will keep trying to wake you. In every sense. Imperilment is bottomless. As long as you are breathing you can always be more scared. But no. They were what they were. Whatever they were. I never saw them as supernatural. In the end there was nothing to be afraid of. I'd already learned that there were things in my life that were best not to share. From about the age of seven I never mentioned synesthesia again. For instance. I thought it was normal and of course it wasnt. So I shut up about it. Anyway, I knew that something was coming, I just didnt know what. Ultimately you will accept your life whether you understand it or not. If I had any fear of the eidolons it was not their being or their appearance but what they had in mind. That I'd no understanding of. The only thing I actually understood about them was that they were trying to put a shape and a name to that which had none. And of course I didnt trust them. Maybe we should move on.

But they come and go at will?

At will?

Yes.

Jesus. I cant answer your question. The only will they subtend would be something like Schopenhauer's Will.

I was just trying to point out that it is unusual for patients to be comfortable with hallucinations. They usually understand that they represent some sort of disruption of reality and that can only be frightening to them.

Them.

Yes.

Well. I guess what I understand is that at the core of the world of the deranged is the realization that there is another world and that they are not a part of it. They see that little is required of their keepers and much of them.

Do you think that's true?

No. But they do.

These beings that come to entertain you but they're not very good at it. Entertain. Distract. What do you think it is that they're supposed to be doing?

I dont know what it is that they're supposed to be doing. It's all lame beyond words.

You must have some notion of what it is that they want.

They want to do something with the world that you havent thought of. They want to set it at question.

Why would they?

Because that's who they are. What they are. If you just wanted an affirmation of the world you wouldnt need to conjure up weird beings.

Is that the purpose of entertainment? If you can call it that. To raise doubts about the world?

Why not?

What else can you say about them? Do they cast a shadow? Can they enter a locked room?

They dont have any trouble putting in an appearance. It wouldnt occur to you to ask if a figure in a dream could cast a shadow.

No. I guess it wouldnt. But you say they're not like figures in a dream.

No. And you might suppose that they devote a certain amount of energy just to appearing plausible. But that's just a charade. A distraction.

From what?

We're sort of back to square one. I suppose it's true that the first duty of any hallucination is to appear real, but to attempt to emulate a reality in which your credentials have expired implies another agenda. To suit yourself up in this new world is at best but a preparation.

You called them hallucinations.

I'm just trying to live in your world.

Now I know you're being facetious.

Do you really want to go into all this?

I'm not sure what all this is.

That there is little joy in the world is not just a view of things. Every benevolence is suspect. You finally figure out that the world does not have you in mind. It never did.

Most people manage to live out their allotted days in something other than a state of despair.

Yes. They do.

If you had to say something definitive about the world in a single sentence what would that sentence be?

It would be this: The world has created no living thing that it does not intend to destroy.

I suppose that's true. What then? Is that all that the world has in mind?

If the world has a mind then it's all worse than we thought.

Does it? It is?

I dont know that we'll get that far.

In these consultations.

Yes. Let's go back to the allotted days.

All right.

I doubt that anyone would live his life over. They'd hardly relive a day of it.

I can think of days I wouldnt mind living over.

Moments of joy or insight maybe. But the whole twenty-four hours?

I wouldnt rule it out. Do you spend a lot of time thinking about death?

I dont know what a lot is. Contemplating death is supposed to have a certain philosophical value. Palliative even. Trivial to say, I suppose, but the best way to die well is to live well. To die for another would give your death meaning. Ignoring for the time being the fact that the other is going to die anyway.

I dont know how much of this is said for effect.

Let's just say all of it.

That, for instance. What about living for others?

Well. Exempting the amorphous others of social ideologies and sticking to real people I suppose it might be rare enough to qualify at least as a neurosis. What do you think?

Or that. There's a note in your files to the effect that you felt you were decaying. I think that's the word you used. Do you remember making such a statement? It sounds like a rather classical somatic delusion. Something out of the literature. Or were you just stringing your keepers along?

Maybe I was just bored.

Well. People get bored.

No they dont.

They dont?

No. They've no idea what boredom is.

Well. I'll take your word for it. Although intelligence in itself is generally supposed to stand off tedium.

I think it does. Up to a point. Then the door buckles.

I guess what concerns me is that the skepticism of these clinicians—some of whom apparently refused in the end to believe anything you said—makes it hard, or maybe even impossible, to treat you. They dont really know what tack to take with someone whom they believe to be simply making everything up.

Making everything up.

Yes.

That troublesome phrase.

Yes.

I suppose I could ask what it is that they think they're being paid to do. They want to explain either my delusions or my predilection for lying but the truth is that they cant explain anything at all. Do they think it would be easier to treat someone who was delusional or someone who only believed that she was? You should listen to what this sounds like. Anyway, I'm long past explaining. I'm done.

Do you feel that you belong here? At Stella Maris?

No. But that doesnt answer your question. The only social entity I was ever a part of was the world of mathematics. I always knew that was where I belonged. I even believed it took precedence over the universe. I do now.

Over the universe.

Yes.

You're not having fun with me.

Not much.

I meant in the sense of pulling my leg.

I know in what sense you meant.

I guess I'm just surprised that you would feel at home in a mental facility.

Maybe it's not a matter of being at home. Maybe it's just a matter of taking advantage of the latitude extended to the deranged.

You talk to the other patients.

Yes. Of course.

Do you think that they tell you the truth?

About what?

Just in general. About anything.

I dont know. No. What I do think is that everybody here pretty much agrees that everybody else who's here should be here. Where else do you get that?

I see.

You should really try to stop saying that.

I'll see what I can do. Your familiars. I really dont know what to call them.

Familiars is okay.

Do they enjoy a certain ascendancy? I'm not clear about this. Do they tell you what to do?

No. The ascendancy they enjoy is that they know who I am but I dont know who they are.

Does that pretty much define the relationship would you say?

Maybe it's simply a model of the relationship in which one stands to the world.

That translates as the world knowing who you are but not you it. Do you believe that?

No. I think your experience of the world is largely a shoring up against the unpleasant truth that the world doesnt know you're here. And no I'm not sure what that means. I think the more spiritual view seeks grace in anonymity. To be celebrated is to set the table for grief and despair. What do you think?

I dont know.

It's not something people ask. It's just what they wonder: Is the world in fact aware of us. But it has good company. As a question. How about: Do we deserve to exist? Who said that it was a privilege? The alternative to being here is not being here. But again, that really means not being here anymore. You cant never have been here. There would be no you to not have been. What do you think, Doctor?

You can call me Michael if you prefer.

I dont. Prefer.

But you dont mind if I call you Alicia.

No.

Your name was originally Alice.

My father's sense of humor.

I'm sorry?

Bob and Alice are the names of the two characters in certain questions of a narrative type in science. I changed it. When I was fifteen.

Your name.

Yes.

You had it changed legally.

Yes.

Wouldnt you have to be eighteen to do that?

You would. I changed my birth certificate first.

How did you do that?

My brother had a criminal friend named John Sheddan who had a friend who ran a printshop in Morristown Tennessee that specialized in forging documents. Anyway, I thought Alicia was more pretentious.

You wanted to be pretentious?

You really do sound like Eliza sometimes. I was Alice Western from Wartburg Tennessee and I wanted to be a Hohenzollern princess. Maybe I am. Wise child.

Maybe we should move on. As you like to say.

All right.

A long silence. Can I ask what you're thinking?

I'm not. Thinking.

There's some question as to whether or not that's possible.

Yes, well. I work at it. You can stop talking to yourself of course. But you can only do so by talking to yourself. Counting your breaths or reciting a mantra. Thinking is harder.

Thinking and talking are different.

Talking is just recording what you're thinking. It's not the thing itself. When I'm talking to you some separate part of my mind is composing what I'm about to say. But it's not yet in the form of words. So what is it in the form of? There's certainly no sense of some homunculus whispering to us the words we're about to say. Aside from raising the spectre of an infinite regress—as in who is whispering to the whisperer—it raises the question of a language of thought. Part of the general puzzle of how we get from the mind to the world. A hundred billion synaptic events clicking away in the dark like blind ladies at their knitting. When you say: How shall

I put this? What is the this that you are trying to put? Maybe we should move on. As you say I like to say.

What would you change if you could change anything?

Anything.

Yes.

I'd elect not to be here.

In this consultation.

On this planet.

You've been placed on suicide watch before. How serious an issue is that?

How serious an issue is suicide?

No. I mean do you think that you're at risk.

I know what you meant. Maybe as long as you're thinking about it you're okay. Once you've made up your mind there's nothing to think about.

So where would you be in this process?

I'd prefer not to be put on suicide watch.

I'd prefer it too.

How many people if they could snap their fingers and vanish would do so? Would you think. All trace of both being and ever having been.

I dont know. Less than you I would suppose.

To wish oneself never to have been. Again, not the same as no longer to be. Who is that? Anaximander? The same for whom?

I've no idea.

You're pretty much obliged to reckon that at the last suspiration the dying become not only acceptant of death but dedicated to it. That there must be some epiphany that makes it possible for even the dullest and most deluded of us to accept not only what is unacceptable but unimaginable. The absolute terminus of the world. Which will not wonder even for the briefest second what might have become of us.

And no comfort I suppose in the commonality of it.

Well. I suppose you could assign some sort of community to the dead. It doesnt seem like much of a community though does it? Unknown to each other and soon to anyone at all. Anyway. It's just that those people who entertain a mental life at odds with that of the general population should be pronounced ipsofuckingfacto mentally ill and in need of medication is ludicrous on the face of it. Mental illness differs from physical illness in that the subject of mental illness is always and solely information.

Information.

Yes. We're here on a need-to-know basis. There is no machinery in evolution for informing us of the existence of phenomena that do not affect our survival. What is here that we dont know about we dont know about. We think.

Would that be the supernatural?

I think it would just be the whereof.

The whereof.

The whereof one cannot speak.

Wittgenstein.

Very good. You're going to run out of breadcrumbs.

The familiars. Now that they've taken a leave of absence does this come as a relief?

God knows. Maybe you imagine I always had it in my power to dismiss them. Or even that they were here at my invitation. And if that were true would I even know it.

Why not?

Maybe because inviting chimeras into your house is a knottier business than inviting neighbors in for tea. Or inviting them to leave. Of course having been asked to leave, the neighbors know that they're not coming back. Which leaves them with a greater freedom to make off with the silver. What can a chimera make off with? I dont know. What did he bring? What did he bring that he might very well leave behind? The fact that he may be composed of vapor doesnt mean that when he leaves your house it will be the same as before he arrived.

Did you ever call the Thalidomide Kid that to his face?

Yes. Once.

What did he say?

He said: Jesus, Jessica. You really take the cake.

Did he really say that?

He really said that.

Do you have a relationship with your family now?

I only have my grandmother.

I thought you had an uncle?

I do. But he's nuttier nor I am. I think she's going to have to put him in a home. Lately he's taken to defecating in odd and difficult to locate places. He managed somehow or other to shit in the ceiling lamp in the kitchen. For instance. I talk with her on the telephone. If rarely. She considers it an extravagance. When she was growing up in Tennessee only rich people had telephones. I have relatives in Rhode Island on my father's side but I dont really know them.

Why is that?

They thought that my father had married beneath himself. They thought we were all just a bunch of hicks.

Does that bother you?

No. They're a pack of fucking idiots. I guess that means it bothers me, right? I dont know. I never think about them.

When did you last see your grandmother?

About three months ago.

Do you intend to see her again?

You keep fishing, dont you?

I just wondered if you were fond of her.

Very. I lost my mother when I was twelve and she lost her daughter. A common grief is supposed to unite people but she was already beginning to see in me something for which she had no name. She certainly didnt know that the word prodigy comes from the Latin word for monster. But the mental tricks I used to pull as a child werent cute anymore. I loved her. But sometimes I would catch her looking at me in a way that was pretty unsettling. The nuns pushed me ahead in school because I was such a pain in the ass. I never even finished the last two grades of grammar school. I'd pretty much stopped sleeping. I'd walk the road at all hours of the night. It was just a two lane country blacktop and there was never any traffic on it. One night I came back and the kitchen light was on. It was about three oclock in the morning and she was standing in the kitchen door when I came up the driveway. Before I reached the house she'd already turned and gone back up the stairs. I knew that it might be one of the last chances we would have to really talk and I almost called after her but I didnt. I thought that maybe when I got a bit older things would change. I thought about her and her life. About the dreams she must have had for her daughter and the dreams she got. I know that I cried over her more than she ever did over me. And I know that she loved Bobby more than she ever would me but that was all right. It didnt make me love her less. I knew things about her that I'd no right to know. But still I thought that if you had a twelve year old granddaughter who walked the roads at three oclock in the morning probably you should sit her down and talk to her about it. And I knew that she couldnt.

Why couldnt she? I'm not sure I understand.

I dont know what to tell you. How to put it. The simplest explanation I suppose would be that she knew the news would be bad and she didnt want to hear it. To say that she was afraid of me I think is a bit strong. But maybe not. I suppose too that she was afraid that no matter how bad things looked they were probably worse. And of course she was right.

And she raised you after your mother died.

Yes.

How old was your brother? At this time.

He was nineteen.

Your father was still alive.

Yes.

But you didnt see much of him.

No.

Did he come to your mother's funeral?

No.

Really?

Really.

Was that upsetting to you?

No. I didnt go either.

You didnt go to your mother's funeral?

No.

What did your family say? Did your brother go?

Yes. Of course. I was twelve. I was going through a religious crisis. I did not want to sit through a High Mass featuring my mother's coffin in the center aisle of the church. I couldnt.

What did your brother say?

He kissed me on the cheek and whispered to me that he loved me and that it was all right. And then it was.

And then it was.

Yes. Look. It's a broken record. I'm doing this for you, not for me. I was given a letter to deliver and told not to read it. And I read it. And I cant unread it. Time's up.

Oh. Yes. Of course.

II

How have you been?

I'm okay.

I missed you last week.

Yeah, well. You know. Busy.

Busy.

Just kidding.

All right.

All right.

So what's been on your mind?

I dont know. What's your wife like?

My wife.

Yes.

She's Italian. What's she like?

Yes.

She's attractive. She likes Bach. She likes Italian food. She works with deaf children.

Is she a good cook?

Yes.

She's not Jewish.

She is Jewish.

She's nice.

Very nice.

Something you're not telling me.

We were divorced. For three years. Then we remarried.

You treated her badly.

Yes. I did.

Why did you?

Because I was an idiot.

That's what Oppenheimer said. At the hearings.

He seems a strange candidate for idiocy.

I think that's why the quote is memorable. People who knew Einstein, Dirac, von Neumann, said that he was the smartest man they'd ever met.

Oppenheimer.

Yes.

I assume your father knew him.

My father worked for him.

What was his opinion?

Of Oppenheimer.

Yes.

He found him engaging, charming, erudite. An excellent party host. A bit frightening.

Frightening?

Yes.

In what sense?

He thought that Oppenheimer's intelligence was not entirely contained. That he was capable of making bad decisions.

Was he?

Yes.

But not Satanic.

That would be a stretch.

I'm assuming that Satan is not a part of your worldview. Even if you seem to acknowledge something very like evil in the scheme of things. You mentioned Chesterton's comment.

Well. I've never seen Satan. That doesnt mean he might not show up. What Chesterton doesnt comment on are the peculiarly material interests of God. If you were a wholly spiritual being why would you dabble in the material at all? At judgment day the bodies rise? What is that about? Spirits are disembodied, not unembodied? Christ ascends into heaven as presumably a corporeal being. Encumbering the godhead with a thing it had not previously to endure. It's hard to know what to make of such lunacy. You can see why Chesterton would steer clear of it.

Was this part of the spiritual crisis that you spoke of?

It's just a commentary. The spiritual nature of reality has been the principal preoccupation of mankind since forever and it's not going away anytime soon. The notion that everything is just stuff doesnt seem to do it for us.

Does it do it for you?

That's the rub, isnt it?

You grew up in Los Alamos.

Yes. We lived there until my mother died. Well. She actually died in Tennessee.

Do you remember Los Alamos?

Yes. Of course.

How old were you when you left?

Eleven.

Eleven.

Yes.

What was it like?

Los Alamos.

Yes.

During the war I think it was pretty primitive. Supposedly there were eight thousand fire extinguishers and five bathtubs. And endless mud. What I remember mostly is people at our house talking until three oclock in the morning.

You were awake until three oclock in the morning.

Yes. The house smelled of perfume and cigarette smoke. You could hear the clink of glasses. I would lie there listening until the last guest left.

You couldnt have understood what they were talking about.

What I understood was that I had to learn what it was that they were talking about.

Do you remember your earliest thoughts?

All I had were thoughts.

I'm not sure I understand.

I understood I was in a place where I was going to be for a long time and that I had to figure it out. That everything depended on my finding out where I was. It wasnt that I thought there could be some other place to be. The world as an absolute was clear to me. But I had to know what it was.

Was this out of fear?

Yes.

Quick answer.

Children are fearful creatures.

How old were you when you discovered mathematics?

Probably older than memory. I was musical first. I had perfect pitch. Have. Later I suppose I came to see the world as pretty much proof against any comprehensive description of it. But music seemed to always stand as an exception to everything. It seemed sacrosanct. Autonomous. Completely self-referential and coherent in every part. If you wanted to describe it as transcendent we could talk about transcendence but we probably wouldnt get very far. I was deeply synesthetic and I thought that if music had an inherent reality—color and taste—that only a few people could identify, then perhaps it had other attributes yet to be discerned. The fact that these things were subjective in no way marked them as imaginary. I'm not doing this very well, am I?

I'm still listening.

If you stretched a piece of music—so to speak—as the tone drew away the color would fade. I've no idea where to put that.

So where does music come from?

No one knows. A platonic theory of music just muddies the water. Music is made out of nothing but some fairly simple rules. Yet it's true that no one made them up. The rules. The notes themselves amount to almost nothing. But why some particular arrangement of these notes should have such a profound effect on our emotions is a mystery beyond even the hope of comprehension. Music is not a language. It has no reference to anything other than itself. You can name the notes with the letters of the alphabet if you like but it doesnt change anything. Oddly, they are not abstractions. Is music as we know it complete? In what sense? Are there classes such as major and minor we've yet to discover? It seems unlikely, doesnt it? Still, lots of things are unlikely until they appear. And what do these categories signify? Where did they come from? What does it mean that they are two shades of blue? In my eyes. If music was here before we were, for whom was it here? Schopenhauer says somewhere that if the entire universe should vanish the only thing left would be music.

That's pretty bold. Did he believe that?

Probably not.

Do you?

I think he was just trying to establish its primacy. Music. As a transcendent phenomenon? A thing which can exist with no assistance?

Can a thing exist with no assistance?

Logically no. If space contained but a single entity the entity would not be there. There would be nothing there for it to be there to.

I dont understand.

It's not important. That's a classical world anyway.

How long has all this been a concern of yours?

I dont know. I'm not sure what memory means. For one thing. One of the problems is that each memory is the memory of the memory before. You cant remember the occasion of the actual memory. How would you do that? You just remember remembering it. And only the most recent memory at that.

I dont know that I follow you.

When I got to high school the first place I went was to the library. It was just a small room with a desk and maybe a thousand books. Maybe not that. But among them was a volume of Berkeley. I dont know what it was doing there. Probably because Berkeley was a bishop. Well. Almost certainly because Berkeley was a bishop. But I sat in the floor and I read *A New Theory of Vision*. And it changed my life. I understood for the first time that the visual world was inside your head. All the world, in fact. I didnt buy into his theological speculations but the physiology was beyond argument. I sat there for a long time. Just letting it soak in. It was hard to avoid the sense that the visual world is the creation of beings with the eyes to do so. Not created out of nothing but out of that something whose actual reality is forever unknowable. Kant. And it is not the case that we can verify the reality of the visual world by reaching out and touching it. For instance. How could it have some contradictory reality? If we were in possession of senses that were in disagreement with one another we wouldnt even be here.

I think I'm going to have to mull this over. In the meantime I have to say that you must be aware that other people get through this same realization as to where the visual world actually occurs— in the visual cortex as opposed to out there in the world—without losing the reality of the world over it.

It wasnt that simple. What followed through the door was a world that had been waiting in the wings ten million years. By the time I got up off the floor of the library I was another person.

Do you feel that you're alone in the world?

Yes. Dont you?

No. I dont. These entertainers that began to appear in your room. Were they a part of this world?

I dont know. One theory is that their purpose was rather to deflect that world.

One theory?

Sure.

What else?

Where to begin.

In the beginning.

In the beginning was the word.

But you dont believe that.

One of the things I realized was that the universe had been evolving for countless billions of years in total darkness and total silence and that the way that we imagine it is not the way that it was. In the beginning always was nothing. The novae exploding silently. In total darkness. The stars, the passing comets. Everything at best of alleged being. Black fires. Like the fires of hell. Silence. Nothingness. Night. Black suns herding the planets through a universe where the concept of space was meaningless for want of any end to it. For want of any concept to stand it against. And the question once again of the nature of that reality to which there was no witness. All of this until the first living creature possessed of vision agreed to imprint the universe upon its primitive and trembling sensorium and then to touch it with color and movement and memory. It made of me an overnight solipsist and to some extent I am yet.

How old were you?

Twelve.

You never graduated from high school.

No. I got a scholarship to the University of Chicago and packed my bags and left. I wonder now at how unconcerned I was. My grandmother drove me to the Greyhound bus station in Knoxville. She was crying and after the bus pulled out I realized that she thought she would never see me again.

You look sad saying that.

I am sad saying that.

Did you have any friends in high school?

One or two. Kids that no one else paid any attention to.

Did you want friends?

Yes. I just didnt know how to get them. I thought maybe when I got to college that that would be my window.

Was it?

I made a few friends. But still I wasnt that social. I wasnt that good at it. I didnt like parties and I didnt like being hit on.

Hit on. What, propositioned?

Yes.

Were you interested in boys?

I was interested in one boy. But it wasnt reciprocal.

Why? He wasnt gay.

No. It was a different sort of problem.

He was older.

Everybody was older. That wasnt the issue.

What was the issue?

Something else.

Okay. What became of the familiars when you got to college?

They showed up about two weeks later. They came on the bus.

Do you really believe that they came on the bus?

Do I really believe that they came on the bus.

All right. Have you ever talked to the Kid about these issues?

I have.

I take it without any sort of conclusion.

No.

I suppose there is no conclusion. Do you consider the Kid a friend?

In the end he was about the only friend I had. And then there were none. But the day I realized that if the Kid were not in my life I would miss him came as a shock to me. What are you writing?

Just a note to myself. Is that all right?

Sure. Pick up milk. Call mother.

Do you want to see it?

No.

You're sure? I dont mind.

I'm sure.

You think sometimes I dont listen.

I think you listen. I'm not so sure what you hear.

You have friends here. At Stella Maris. What about them?

Yes, well. Sometimes I'll pick out somebody in the dayroom and just sit down and start talking to them.

What do they say?

Usually nothing. But sometimes they'll start talking about what's on their mind and then in the middle of their disquisition they'll make a reference to something I said. Much in the way you might incorporate some sound in the night into your dream. And I have to say that to see my thoughts sorted into their monologue can be a bit unsettling. I would like to belong but I dont. And they know that. A dozen psychiatrists recently got themselves admitted to various mental institutions. It was an experiment. They just said they heard voices and were immediately diagnosed as schizoid. But the inmates were onto them. They looked them over and told them they werent crazy. That they were reporters or something. Then they just walked away.

You would like to belong?

I'm not here as an experiment. I can put any spin on it I like but in the end this is where I am.

I find that a somewhat odd comment.

I'm a somewhat odd girl. Play the tape back. You'll hear it differently.

How aware are you of the fact that you're extremely good-looking?

Are you trying to fuck me, Doctor?

No. I've never had a relationship with a patient. Anyway, infidelity is a thing of the past for me. Have you had many counselors try to seduce you?

I think seduce might be a somewhat fanciful description of their efforts.

Have any tried to rape you?

Yes. One.

What did you do?

I told him that my brother would come to kill him. That he could count his life in hours.

Is that true? About your brother?

Yes.

Without question.

Without question.

Berkeley. Did reading him extend your skepticism about reality?

I'm not sure I know what that means.

If anything.

If anything. It made me question my understanding of reality, yes. But it also made the philosophical history of inquiry more credible to me. It made epistemology a legitimate discipline. I think it even made me see the fraudulence of the queries it itself had engendered.

Reality is always the subject.

Pretty much.

Is it knowable?

Oh boy.

I'll take that back. What is it that we dont know that you wish that we did?

You mean aside from the old standards that dont have answers.

Who are we, why are we here, why is there something rather than nothing.

Yes.

Do you want to take a shot at any of those? How about something rather than nothing?

The notion of nothing is an inconceivable notion.

Do you still study physics?

No.

What's a gluon?

A conceivable notion.

Is it a force or a particle?

A particle. Although at that scale the distinction is not so clear.

What does it do?

It carries the news from quark to quark. It's not that complicated. An atom is composed of smaller particles. Nucleons. And these particles are composed of quarks. Generally three. The quarks have dumb names. Top quark and bottom quark. Up and down quarks. A positron is made of two up quarks and a down quark. A neutron is made of two down quarks and an up quark. And so on. It all works. No one is quite sure why. But the gluon is what keeps the particles informed.

Why is quantum mechanics called quantum mechanics?

Because it explains mechanisms. Among physicists the accent is on quantum. It states the type of mechanics that it is. It's not quantum *mechanics*.

All right.

You look dubious.

No. It's all right. Why is it so weird? Supposedly.

Nobody knows.

I mean in what way is it weird.

I know. There are a number of things you can talk about. Feynman says that all of quantum weirdness is already there in the two-slit experiment. He's probably right. He usually is. The experiment, repeated ad whatever, shows that a single particle can go through two separate apertures at the same time.

Do you believe that?

Most fervently.

And this is a part of quantum mechanics.

It is.

A well-thought-of physical theory.

Yes. It's the most successful physical theory ever devised. It's the theory of small particles. Atoms and smaller. Or so it is commonly thought. But that may just be bad math. Some physicists suspect that the theory must eventually arrive at the understanding that the universe itself is a quantum phenomenon. That what quantum mechanics ultimately describes is the universe.

Do you suspect that?

Yes. I'm among the suspicious.

What else.

What else?

Is weird.

Experiments, gedanken or actual, seem to require our active involvement. If we're not there they dont work. The ugly truth is that other than Feynman's sum-over theories there is no believable explanation of quantum mechanics that does not involve human consciousness. Of course this raises the question as to how it managed to get along without us before we were invented. But it's not that simple. I think what is being pointed out is that human consciousness and reality are not the same thing. Which we've known for a long time. Even if we're not all that sure about Kant. In this instance. Anyway, you cant ignore the evidence of the experiments. Everything from the two slits to all those strange doings with Stern-Gerlach magnets in which fairly bright scientists find themselves unable to outwit a sodium particle. It's a popular notion in some quarters that these inquiries are just philosophy. And the popular answer to them is just shut up and calculate.

That's not you.

No. All of these calculations produce partial differential equations. The truth of the universe is on the other side of those equations.

What do the physicists say about this?

Not much. Mostly they roll their eyes. They're not Kantian sorts of guys. The problem with the unknowable absolute is that if you could actually say something about it it wouldnt be the unknowable absolute anymore. You can get from the noumenal to the phenomenal without stirring from your chair. In other words, nothing can be excerpted from the absolute without being rendered perceptual. Bearing in mind that to claim reality for what is unknowable is already to speak in tongues. The trouble with the perfect and objective world—Kant's or anybody's—is that it is unknowable by definition. I love physics but I dont confuse it with absolute reality. It is our reality. Mathematical ideas have a considerable shelflife. Do they exist in the absolute? How is that possible? I said to myself. But then myself became another self. No more than right. It took the math with it. The idea. A long period of uncertainty. When I recohered I was someplace else. As if I had escaped my own lightcone. Into what used to be called the absolute elsewhere.

I dont understand.

I know. Me either. It's just that my view was that you cant fetch something out of the absolute without fetching it out of the absolute. Without converting it into the phenomenological. By which it then becomes our property with our fingerprints all over it and the absolute is nowhere to be found. Now I'm not so sure.

Can we talk about the Kid?

Sure. What the fuck.

I've touched a nerve.

Not really. I just felt like being rude.

What does he look like?

He's three feet two. He has an odd face. Odd look I guess you would say. No particular age. He has these flippers. He's balding if not bald. He would weigh maybe fifty pounds. You're smiling.

I was thinking about him stepping into Charon's boat.

Yes. I'd thought about that. Dante doesnt think about it until he himself steps into the boat and feels it settle.

I didnt know that.

Yeah well. Sorry about the fuck.

We'll live with it. How do you know that he's three feet two?

I measured him.

He stood still for that?

No. I measured him the way Thales measured the Pyramids. I made a note of the length of his shadow on the carpet and compared it to the length of my own and the relative lengths of our shadows were equivalent to our respective heights.

Why did you want to know his exact height?

I think I just wanted to know if he had one.

What else?

He has no eyebrows. He looks a bit scarred. Maybe burnt. His skull is scarred. As if maybe he'd had an accident. Or a difficult birth. Whatever that might mean. He wears a sort of kimono. And he paces all the time. With his flippers behind his back. Sort of like an iceskater. He talks all the time and he uses idioms that I'm sure he doesnt understand. As if he'd found the language somewhere and wasnt all that sure what to do with it. In spite of that—or maybe because of it—he'll sometimes say something quite striking. But he's hardly a dream figure. He is coherent in every detail. He is perfect. He is a perfect person.

Personage. I thought you said.

Personage then.

Going back a few years. The fact that Thorazine stopped the visits of these familiars. Doesnt that suggest to you something about the nature of their reality?

Or my ability to perceive it.

Well. I suppose one could say that.

I suppose one could. One just did. Drugs alter perception. To conform to what? I used to have somewhat firmer convictions about the whole business. But one's convictions as to the nature of reality must also represent one's limitations as to the perception of it. And then I just stopped worrying about it. I accepted the fact that I would die without really knowing where it was that I had been and that was okay. Well. Almost. I told Leonard that reality was at best a collective hunch. But that was just a line I stole from a female comedian.

Leonard?

He's a friend here.

Did he laugh?

No. He took it pretty seriously.

The Kid once told you that other people could see him? Did you say that?

Some other people.

What do you think that means?

I dont know. You're the psychiatrist.

You wont see him again. The Kid.

You're fishing again.

But you said goodbye to him.

Yes.

What did he say?

Not much. He wanted to know if I would miss him.

If you would miss him.

Yes. He recited a poem to me. Which was a surprise. I dont know what it means.

Do you remember how it went?

Yes. Pretty quickly.

I meant do you remember the poem.

I know what you meant.

I guess I should just ask if you would say it.

No. I wont.

All right. The idea of the Kid as some sort of an evil djinn—

which I take it to have been the view of most of your counselors—is not your view. Or maybe you would say that it is just not the case.

Not the case. No.

But could you say how you do see him?

I think the way I see him is the case. Isnt it?

All right.

You're not really asking me about the Kid. You're asking me about me. And I cant tell you what you want to know. Even if I could I probably wouldnt.

All right. Sorry.

No need. Do you know the Tractatus? You knew where the whereof was from.

I've looked at it. I couldnt make much of it.

I think the case with the Kid is that he was just doing the best he could. Like everybody else.

Do you see him as benign?

If I see him as benign it's because I know what else is out there.

And of which I—for instance—would probably not be aware.

Let's just say that I'd be surprised.

What do you think of people? Just in general.

Is that actually a question?

Why not?

I guess I try not to. Think of them.

Is that true?

No. I think that there is love in my heart. It just shows up as pity. I imagine that I've seen the horror of the world but I know that's not true. Still, you cant put back what you've seen. There has never been a century so grim as this one. Does anyone seriously think that we've seen the last of its like? And yet what can the world's troubles mean to someone unable to shoulder her own?

Sometimes everything?

Yes. I think you could be right.

I'm sorry. I didnt mean to upset you.

I'm not upset. There's more where that came from.

Maybe we should take a break.

Okay.

———

Are you all right?

I'm okay.

We still have twenty minutes.

I know. Fire away.

What is it that you like to do? What do you enjoy?

That sounds like something out of the book. What's the weirdest answer you ever got?

I'm not sure I could say. But patients will surprise you.

Would they surprise Krafft-Ebing?

I meant in a good way. They sometimes have rather sophisticated interests. Although I have to say that they're often inclined to give up what they treasure for what makes them miserable. Your principal interest other than mathematics would have been music.

Yes.

How good a violinist were you?

Pretty good. I could never have been a concert violinist.

You werent that good.

I wouldnt practice. I didnt play for weeks at a time. You cant do that.

You werent that interested.

No. I loved it. But I loved mathematics more. I've probably spent twenty thousand hours at math.

That's a lot of hours.

Yes.

Do you remember all of it?

Yes. You have to.

What else.

I dont know. Pick something from your list.

Do you think your relationship with your mother might have had anything to do with this?

You're making an Eliza joke.

Yes. Anyway, I've wanted to ask you your opinion of psychiatrists. As in how bad is it.

Is that on the list?

Why not?

I always thought that in order to want to do psychiatry you would have to be a bit shaky yourself. If your view of the deranged is too clinical you're at a disadvantage. On the other hand you cant just be bonkers.

You always thought.

Yes.

And now?

What's the point?

You probably know them better than I do.

I dont know. I guess I dont see you hanging out with a bunch of shrinks. But then I dont know who you do hang with.

I suppose I do find the patients more interesting than the doctors.

Me too.

You dont see what we do as science.

No. The docs seem to pretty much avoid neuroscience. Down there with lantern and clipboard roaming the sulci. Sulcuses? Easy to see why. If a psychosis was just some synapses misfiring why wouldnt you simply get static? But you dont. You get a carefully crafted and fairly articulate world never seen before. Who's doing this? Who is it who is running around hooking up the dangling wires in new and unusual ways. Why is he doing it? What is the algorithm he follows? Why do we suspect there is one?

I've no idea.

The docs dont seem to consider the care with which the world of the mad is assembled. A world which they imagine themselves questioning when of course they are not. The alienist skirts the edges of lunacy as the priest does sin. Stalled at the door of his own mandate. Studying with twisted lip a reality that has no standing. Alien nation. Ask another question. Devise a theory. The enemy of your undertaking is despair. Death. Just like in the real world. You're not buying this.

I'm listening.

Sixteen minutes.

You're trying to find some way to fill them?

No. I can stop whenever I like.

And so can we all.

Rather Chaucerian that. And so can we all.

You dont think the therapist has all that much capacity for healing.

I think what most people think. That it's caring that heals, not theory. Good the world over. And it may even be that in the end all problems are spiritual problems. As moonminded as Carl Jung was he was probably right about that. Keeping in mind that the German language doesnt distinguish between mind and soul. As for the institutions, you have a sense that a place like Stella Maris was prepared with a certain amount of thought. They just didnt know who was coming. I think the care here is pretty good, but like care everywhere it can never keep up with the need. After so many years even the bricks are poisoned. There are remedies but there is no remedy. Sites that have been host to extraordinary suffering will eventually be either burned to the ground or turned into temples.

Are all your views so somber?

I dont consider them somber. I think they're simply realistic. Mental illness is an illness. What else to call it? But it's an illness associated with an organ that might as well belong to Martians for all our understanding of it. Aberrant behavior is probably a mantra. It hides more than it reveals. Among the problems the therapist faces is that the patient may have no desire to be healed. Tell me, Doctor, what will I then be like?

Do the mad have a sense of justice?

Is that a serious question? They're seething. Injustice is their main preoccupation. I think your eyes are beginning to glaze over.

I'm all right. You never look at the clock, do you?

I dont have to.

How are we doing? Timewise.

Marvelous thought, that. Time wise. We have fourteen minutes. The days are long but the years are short.

Is there a part of your life that one might characterize as unstable and yet has nothing to do with the . . . what? Horts?

Let me see if I can rephrase that for you.

Sure.

I'll do it for free. Am I crazy all the time or only when my little friends are around.

Okay.

I dont know what that means. I dont think the Kid doesnt exist when I dont see him. For instance. A quantum mechanical Kid. Maybe we should move on.

Okay. What is there that's important about you that I dont know?

Is that out of the book?

I dont think so.

I'm a lesbian.

I dont think so.

How do you know?

I just know. You flirt with me. For one thing.

You think I find you attractive.

Yes. I would have to say yes.

Well. I'm sorry. It's not really about flirting.

What is it about?

Maybe it's just about having no one in your life. About coming to terms with the fact that whatever it is that you are going to say goodbye to it's not going to say goodbye back.

Have you talked to your grandmother about your brother?

Yes. I had to tell her.

What did she say?

She started crying. She kept saying his name.

Did she say anything else?

She asked me if I was calling from Italy.

Is she going to go to Italy?

No. She wouldnt know how to do that.

You could take her.

No. I couldnt.

All right.

But it's not all right. Is it?

If you dont want to talk about your brother I can understand that. I dont know. Did you say anything to him? Did you think he might be able to hear you?

I told him I would rather be dead with him than alive without him.

I'll take that as a forewarning.

Your life is set upon you like a dog.

Is that a quote?

Not that I know of.

Not Jewish anyway.

No.

Do you have any Jewish family connections?

No. We didnt grow up Jewish.

But you knew you were Jewish.

No. I knew something. Anyway, my forebears counting coppers out of a clackdish are what have brought me to this station in life. Jews represent two percent of the population and eighty percent of the mathematicians. If those numbers were even a little more skewed we'd be talking about a separate species.

Isnt that a bit farfetched?

No. It's not fetched far enough. You can have separate histories in the same house. Darwin's question remains unanswered. How do we come by mental abilities that have no history? How is it that the brain seems to prepare for what's coming? No idea. How much of the brain's circuitry is undedicated, simply awaiting the arrival of new opportunities? Any? How does making change in the market prepare one's grandchildren for quantum mechanics? For topology?

Grandchildren?

You can fill in the greats.

I dont know. I'm not sure that I'm following you. Why dont we get back to you?

This is me.

Your personal history. Where were you before you came here?

In the dayroom.

You're being a smart aleck.

I was in Italy. Waiting for my brother to die.

How long were you there?

Two months. A little more.

They waited two months to ask your permission to terminate life support?

No. They just got more insistent.

Did you speak Italian?

I do okay. Anyway, maybe that's what he would have wanted. I dont know. I only knew that I couldnt do it. I ran for my life.

Are you all right with that?

No. Good God.

When you arrived here you had quite a lot of money.

Not that much. My brother and I had inherited money from our paternal grandmother. When he gave me my share there wasnt really anything that I wanted. So I bought this rather extraordinary Amati. I knew the instrument. I'd seen it in two books and of course in the Christie catalog. The last time it was sold was in 1863 and I figured it wouldnt be coming on the market again anytime soon.

A violin.

Yes.

How expensive a violin are we talking about?

I paid a little over two hundred thousand dollars for it.

That's impressive. How much money had you inherited?

My share was something over a half million dollars. I thought the violin was a good idea. Even if I did worry about leaving it in my room. I used to keep it under the pillow. For a while I actually kept the money in a shoebox in the closet.

You had the money in cash?

Yes. When my brother found out he made me rent a safe deposit box.

You didnt consider investing it?

We'd inherited the money and we didnt owe any taxes on it. But we couldnt prove that. It was buried in my grandmother's basement. She told us where it was and that we were to have it. But of course there wasnt any documentation for it.

She'd buried the money in her basement.

Our grandfather had. It was in twenty dollar goldpieces. Stacked in lengths of lead pipe.

This is turning into a fairly curious tale.

People do curious things.

Christie's. You bought the violin at auction?

Yes. I bought it through Bein & Fushi. In Chicago. They werent really even in business yet. But they acted as my agents.

They wouldnt have had an instrument like that in stock.

No. They didnt have any stock. They were a brand-new company.

I can see how you would be concerned about it.

When a Cremona is stolen it can be stolen forever. One more of a handful that might never be found. I'd thought about painting it. Some sort of water soluble paint that would be easy to get off without damaging the finish. Paint it gold, maybe. Put it in a cheap case. But I thought about the quotation that Quine cites. Save the surface and you save all. Anyway I knew I couldnt bring myself to do it.

Who's Quine?

He's a philosopher. Some say the greatest living.

Do you?

Maybe. Of course he thinks he understands mathematics. Cant seem to leave it alone.

But that's a quote, you said.

Yes. It's in the frontispiece of one of his books.

Does he give an attribution?

Yes. Sherwin-Williams.

The paint company.

Yes.

You're joking.

No. I'm not. Neither was Quine. Well. Maybe a little. Maybe quite a bit now that I think about it.

Bein & Fushi. Do I have that right?

Yes. The day I picked it up I took it home on the bus. I climbed the stairs to my room and went in and sat on the bed with it in my lap. Just looking at the case. The case was German. Probably late eighteenth century. It looked almost new. Black calf with German-silver latches. I flipped the latches up with my thumb one by one and raised the lid. I can remember every breath.

But you'd seen it before. You saw it at the dealer's.

No. I hadnt. They put it on the counter and started to unsnap the latches but I stopped them. I'd seen photos of course. The photos in Christie's catalog were probably the best. The maple was really close grained and curly. The back was two-piece and almost book-matched. Very unusual. The finish was pretty much gone from the neck, down to the wood actually, and I thought it could even be original although the catalog didnt say that. I thought it was the most amazing thing I'd ever seen.

You bought it sight unseen.

Yes. I went down to Bein & Fushi with the money in a shopping bag.

On the bus.

Yes. When I gave them the money they took it into the back room and counted it. They'd no idea what to do with it and the auction was in five days. You'd think that you could buy things with cash but apparently it's not that easy anymore. They couldnt believe I was carrying a third of a million dollars around in a shopping bag. I told them I was hiding it in plain sight but that just seemed to confuse them.

A third of a million dollars.

Well, three hundred thousand actually.

What did Christie's think that it would sell for?

I dont think they knew. It was such a unique piece. They were guessing at least two hundred thousand dollars but my guys at Bein & Fushi thought it would go for more.

But you were ready to push the whole three hundred thousand forward.

Yes. I told them to just go ahead and buy it.

It would sell for what it was worth. By definition.

Yes.

And so what did it go for?

Two-thirty.

Where was the auction? In New York?

Yes.

And you told them that you didnt even want to see it.

Yes.

I'm guessing that they already thought you were a bit strange.

I dont know what they thought. They got a nice commission out of it. They tried to give me a check for the remainder of the money but I told them cash only. Bobby's rule.

What did they say to that?

They rolled around in the floor gurgling and calling out to one another.

All right. You didnt want to see it because you just wanted to be alone with it when you did see it.

Yes.

So you took it home on the bus.

Yes. When I got home I sat down on the bed with it in my lap and opened the case. Nothing smells like a three hundred year old violin. I plucked the strings and it was surprisingly close. I took it out of the case and sat there and tuned it. I wondered where the Italians had gotten ebony wood. For the pegs. And the fingerboard of course. The tailpiece. I got out the bow. It was German made. Very nice ivory inlays. I tightened it and then I just sat there and started playing Bach's Chaconne. The D Minor? I cant remember. Such a raw, haunting piece. He'd composed it for his wife who'd died while he was away. But I couldnt finish it.

Why not?

Because I just started crying. I started crying and I couldnt stop.

Why were you crying? Why are you crying?

I'm sorry. For more reasons than I could tell you. I remember blotting the tears off of the spruce top of the Amati and laying it aside and going into the bathroom to splash water on my face. But it just started again. I kept thinking of the lines: What a piece of work is a man. I couldnt stop crying. And I remember saying: What are we? Sitting there on the bed holding the Amati, which was so beautiful it hardly seemed real. It was the most beautiful thing I'd ever seen and I couldnt understand how such a thing could even be possible.

Do you want to stop?

Yes. I'm sorry.

III

Good morning. How have you been?

Never better.

I'm sure you're being facetious. Are you okay?

Yes.

Is there anything from our last meeting that you'd like to go over?

No. You dont have your folder.

I pretty much know what's in it. I thought we might just begin.

Okay.

What would you like to talk about?

Bell's Inequality.

I'm sorry?

You say. I dont care. The weather.

Tell me about your father.

Eliza.

Sorry. Is it true that even the people who developed the program would sign up for therapeutic sessions?

So I've heard.

Your father died some time after your mother.

About four years.

After a long illness.

Long enough to kill him.

That sounds a bit harsh.

Look. When you quote lines to me from newspaper obituaries I dont respond well.

Sorry. I'll try to bear that in mind. How old were you?

Fifteen.

Did you see much of him at this time?

No. He was living in a cabin in the mountains. Above Lake Tahoe.

Had you had a falling-out with him?

No.

He was a physicist on the Manhattan Project. Did he ever talk about that?

Mostly with Bobby. This is beginning to sound like a congressional hearing.

Maybe you should just tell me whatever comes to mind.

No. Carry on. I suppose you want to know if he felt guilty about building the bomb. He didnt. But he's dead. And my brother is brain-dead and I'm in the nuthouse.

All right. What else?

What else. He was one of a group of scientists who went into Hiroshima after the war to report on the damage. I think he was sobered by what he saw. I cant really speak for him. Whoever made the bomb was going to blow something up with it and I'm sure he thought better us than them. Whoever them might turn out to be. The arguments about Truman's decision generally center around the loss of life in a land invasion. My father had another take on it. He thought that if Japan had been defeated in a land invasion there would have been no miracle of reconstruction after the war. That Japan would have been humiliated as a nation and would have entered into a long decline. But as it was, they were not defeated in battle. They were defeated by witchcraft.

That doesnt seem a bit self-serving?

If you like. It might also be true.

Do you think that it's true?

I dont know. It's a theory. Invented and patented by my father. I dont have any politics. And I'm pacifist to the bone. Only a nation can make war—in the modern sense—and I dont like nations. I believe in running away. Much as you'd step out of the path of an oncoming bus. If we'd had a child I would take it to where war seemed least probable. Although it's hard to outguess history. But you can try. No I dont, to answer your next question.

You dont blame your father.

No.

You said if we had a child.

If I had a child.

Who's we?

None of your business.

You dont think that your father lost any sleep over the bomb.

My father didnt sleep before the bomb and he didnt sleep after. I think most of the scientists didnt give that much thought to what was going to happen. They were just having a good time. They all said the same thing about the Manhattan Project. That they'd never had so much fun in their lives. But anyone who doesnt understand that the Manhattan Project is one of the most significant events in human history hasnt been paying attention. It's up there with fire and language. It's at least number three and it may be number one. We just dont know yet. But we will.

You think that your father didnt really dwell on the outcome of the project.

I think that he did dwell. And that he was unusual in that. He didnt have a lot of sympathy with all the handwringing that went on after Hiroshima. He was older than most of the scientists. I think the average age was around twenty-six or twenty-seven. I think a few were even in their teens. When they suddenly became peacemongers he just thought they were a bunch of hypocrites. After the war he worked with Teller. They detonated bombs capable of reducing fairly large parcels of the known world to uninhabitable rubble. Everybody hated Teller and they hated my father. Too bad. I dont know what to tell you about his sleep. I never slept either. And I didnt bomb anybody.

You were born at Los Alamos.

Yes. Boxing Day. Nineteen fifty-one.

Boxing Day? What is that?

It's the day after Christmas.

Why is it called Boxing Day?

It's called Boxing Day because that's the day you box up all the crap you got that you dont want and take it back to the store.

That's not true.

No. Traditionally it was the day you exchanged gifts. Boxes of cookies or whatever. An army sergeant drove my mother to the hospital in one of those olivedrab sedans left over from the war. There was nobody else around. She was supposed to go to Tennessee but in the end they wouldnt let her travel.

Where was your father?

He was in Providence. The one in Rhode Island.

Why was he in Providence? He was visiting with his family?

He went to hear Kurt Gödel give the Gibbs Lecture at the American Mathematical Society at Brown University.

He didnt spend Christmas with your mother.

He did not.

Were they estranged?

You'd have to define estranged. I dont think entirely. But then I wasnt there. Anyway, I dont fault him for going to hear Gödel. I would have. Even though Gödel just read the paper in a monotone. The paper was on the foundations of mathematics. Mostly it was a defense of platonism. I dont know that my father was all that interested in the subject but he was interested in Gödel.

Have you read the paper?

Yes. Of course.

Of course?

I've read practically all of Gödel's papers. Most of the notes. Including those written in Gabelsberger.

What is that?

It's the shorthand that Gödel used. In keeping with his other idiosyncrasies. It's nineteenth century German. Maybe eighteenth, I dont know.

How long did it take you to learn it?

Longer than I would have thought. Gödel was smart, but among other things he was a mathematical platonist and I wanted to know why. To me the idea was simply incoherent. But then I didnt really know how smart Gödel was.

Now I'm not even sure I know what that means. Mathematical platonist.

What it sounds like? It's usually called realism nowadays. It supposedly expresses a belief in the existence of mathematical entities independent of the human mind. It's a belief common to older mathematicians and to me it just seemed full of holes. If mathematical objects exist independently of human thought what else are they independent of? The universe, I suppose. When you solve a problem there is always the compelling sense that the solution was there and that you have discovered it. Besides which it has a certain empirical weight to it in that other mathematicians will agree with you that the answer is correct. If it is.

And I suppose this has at least something to do with your understanding of reality in general.

Well. You can spend a lot of time categorizing realities. Their correspondences. We probably dont want to start down that road.

All right. I dont know that much about Gödel. I know that he had a famous theory that mathematics couldnt solve all the questions it posed. Or something like that.

Something like that, yes. Two theorems. In 1931.

Is that a theory you agree with?

Of course. The paper explaining them is brilliant. It's beyond argument. In his later years Gödel drifted away from mathematics into philosophy. Then he went crazy.

How crazy?

Pretty bad. He wouldnt eat. Thought the food was poisoned. When he died he weighed about seventy pounds. Oppenheimer was head of IAS at the time and he would go over to see him in the hospital. One day the doctor came in. He didnt know who Gödel was—just some nutty professor from the university—and Oppenheimer told him to take good care of Gödel because he was the greatest logician since Aristotle. And the doctor nodded and began to edge toward the door and Oppenheimer realized that he was thinking: Good God, now there's two of them.

His theory. Is it true that it cast doubt over the legitimacy of mathematics? Is that why it's famous?

No. That's all nonsense. It may have started with von Neumann. He was present at Gödel's presentation to the Vienna Circle and when Gödel finished reading the papers von Neumann said: It's all over.

Von Neumann said that.

Yes.

But it wasnt.

No. It wasnt. Well, something was over. Not least being a number of Hilbert's problems from 1900.

Von Neumann was a famous mathematician.

This was before he was famous. But he badly wanted to be famous. The reason he made the comment was to show everybody that he'd understood the paper.

But the comment was . . . What was it? Incorrect?

He probably wasnt the only one there who thought that mathematics itself had been brought into question. Sometimes it takes a while to sort things out. Mathematics is constantly being questioned. That's what it's for. Some good mathematicians have left the discipline. Exceeding even the number who have wound up in the madhouse.

Why is that?

I thought that's why we were here.

You no longer do math.

No. Well, maybe on the problem of problems. Which wont go away.

Which is?

The foundational problem. What to do about Frege. The Grundlagen. The beginning and the end. What are we doing and how do we know. An insight. Does something know? Is that possible? And if it does what must we become in order for it to tell us? The Langlands project. Things that are not ever going to tell me what I want to know.

I see.

I dont think so. Mathematics is ultimately a faith-based initiative. And faith is an uncertain business.

I'm not sure I understand. Mathematics as what? A sort of spiritual undertaking?

It's just that I dont have something else to call it. I've thought for a long time that the basic truths of mathematics must transcend number. It is after all a rather ramshackle affair. For all its considerable beauty. The laws of mathematics supposedly derive from the rules of logic. But there is no argument for the rules of logic that does not presuppose them. I suppose one thing that might evoke the analogy with the spiritual is the understanding that the greatest spiritual insights seem to derive from the testimonies of those who stand teetering in the dark.

I dont see how mathematical truths could transcend number.

I know.

But you're nevertheless a fan of Gödel.

Yes. Huge fan. I agree with Oppenheimer's view.

Are most of your heroes mathematicians?

Yes. Or heroines.

Who else do you admire?

It's a long list.

Okay.

Cantor, Gauss, Riemann, Euler. Hilbert. Poincaré. Noether. Hypatia. Klein, Minkowski, Turing, von Neumann. Hardly even a partial list. Cauchy, Lie, Dedekind, Brouwer. Boole. Peano. Church is still alive. Hamilton, Laplace, Lagrange. The ancients of course. You look at these names and the work they represent and you realize that the annals of latterday literature and philosophy by comparison are barren beyond description.

Those names are not familiar to me.

I know.

Are any of them women?

Emmy Noether. She was a great mathematician. One of the greatest. One of the founders of mathematical physics. There are others. Women. No Fields Medals yet of course.

That's the highest honor in mathematics.

Yes.

I'm surprised that your friend Grothendieck is not on your list. Did you forget him?

I dont forget Grothendieck. All the ones I named are dead.

Is that a requirement for greatness?

It's a requirement for not waking up tomorrow morning and saying something extraordinarily stupid. You asked why Grothendieck left mathematics. The notion that this implies lunacy, appealing as that may be, is probably not altogether correct. It would certainly appear to be the case that rewriting most of the mathematics of the past half century has done little to allay his skepticism. Wittgenstein was fond of saying that nothing can be its own explanation. I'm not sure how far that is from saying that things ultimately contain no information concerning themselves. But it may be true that you have to be on the outside looking in. You can ask what is even meant by a description. Is there a better description of a cube than that of its construction? I dont know. What can you say of any attribute other than that it resembles some things and not others? Color. Form. Weight. When you're faced with a class of one you see the problem. It doesnt have to be something grand like time or space. It can be something pretty everyday. The component parts of music. Are there musical objects? Music is composed of notes? Is that right? The complexity of mathematics has shifted it from a description of things and events to the power of abstract operators. At what point are the origins of systems no longer relevant to their description, their operation? No one, however inclined to platonism, actually believes that numbers are requisite to the operation of the universe. They're only good to talk about it. Is that right?

I dont know.

The reason mathematics works—some would argue—is that you're at the end of your tether. You cant mathematicize mathematics. You look dubious.

Sorry.

Even fairly simple animals can count. They understand that three is more than two. They dont know what that means? Neither do I. You asked me about Grothendieck. The topos theory he came up with is a witches' brew of topology and algebra and mathematical logic. It doesnt even have a clear identity. The power of the theory is still speculative. But it's there. You have a sense that it is waiting quietly with answers to questions that nobody has asked yet.

That sounds a bit platonic.

Dont it though? With the refreshingly new and unhappy prospect of our species having created a thing we have yet to discover. The Kid thought Dirac's name was Pamela.

Pamela?

He used to sometimes sign his name PAM Dirac. For Paul Adrien Maurice. Anyway, these are my people. I dont have anyone else.

You look sad. Saying that.

I am sad saying that.

It has to do with intelligence.

Yes. And again, when you're talking about intelligence you're talking about number. A claim that the mathless are quick to frown upon. It's about calculation and the nature of calculation. Verbal intelligence will only take you so far. There is a wall there, and if you dont understand numbers you wont even see the wall. People from the other side will seem odd to you. And you will never understand the latitude which they extend to you. They will be cordial— or not—depending on their nature. Of course one might also add that intelligence is a basic component of evil. The more stupid you are the less capable you are of doing harm. Except perhaps in a clumsy and inadvertent manner. The word cretin comes from the French chrétien. Supposedly if you could think of nothing good to say about a dullard you would say that he was a good Christian. Diabolical on the other hand is all but synonymous with ingenious. What Satan had for sale in the garden was knowledge.

Beauty in mathematics.

Yes.

Is that a part of its description? Is that what makes it true?

Profound equations are often said to be beautiful. Maxwell I suppose. If you overlook the E and B vector potential in place of the A. If you look into the principle of least action you are likely to be left rather solemnly silent.

Are the equations themselves beautiful?

Not if you dont know what they mean.

Is $E = mc^2$ a thing of beauty?

You should see it in color.

Moving on.

Moving.

Was your father a decent person?

I think so. He was kind to me.

He actually worked on the bomb that they dropped on Hiroshima.

Yes. So did my mother.

At Oak Ridge. Your mother.

Yes. At Y-12.

But she didnt really know what she was doing.

Probably not. She sat in front of a meter for eight hours every day. No one was allowed to talk. The day after Hiroshima they knew. If anyone then had a negative opinion about their war work I never heard it. I think they were pretty proud of it. But if you think any of this in turn might have something to do with Edwardian dwarves dancing the Charleston in my bedroom at two oclock in the morning I'd be happy to hear your exposition.

Maybe we should move along.

Okay.

Is it okay?

Sure. You're wearing your dubious face again. What's she saying? What's she hiding? What if it's worse than I thought?

Is it?

Worse?

Yes.

Probably. We keep coming back to my father. It's not that I dont know what the issue is. But maybe we should just table it for now. He's dead and I wish that he wasnt.

How long has your family lived in Wartburg?

Since 1943. We were forced off of our farm by the Project.

Oak Ridge.

Yes. The farm was just outside of Clinton Tennessee. On the Clinch River. We'd been there since the Civil War.

So you would not have ever seen the farm.

By the time I came along it was at the bottom of a lake. My grandmother used to talk about it. The house was the old post and beam construction. The floors were walnut sawed in a streamdriven sashmill that they'd built and she said that there were planks in the parlor—as she called it—that were three feet wide.

So what happened to it?

It was condemned by the US Government. Flattened with bulldozers. In order to build a plant for the enrichment of nuclear fuel.

That's painful for you.

I suppose. At one time. At one time I could have seen myself living there. It was built by my great-grandfather. I've seen photographs of it and it was quite beautiful. They'd never built a house before. I'm not sure they'd ever even seen one built. What if they could have seen eighty years into the future? That's not very long. The simplest undertaking is predicated upon a future that has no warrant.

You said that the Manhattan Project was a major historical event. Is it possible to see it with any sort of perspective? We've been a long time without a nuclear war.

Yes. Well, it's probably like any bankruptcy. The longer you're able to put it off the worse it's going to be. The next great war wont arrive until everyone who remembers the last one is dead.

You think that nuclear war is inevitable.

I agree with Plato that only the dead have seen an end to war. And people dont fight with rocks when they have guns. Etcetera and so on.

We're living in a fool's paradise.

I dont know what we're living in.

All right. Family history. Your mother I take it grew up in that house.

Yes. She did.

But when I asked you about it what you told me was what your grandmother remembered.

My mother was in high school when the war came to town. She may have thought that the world was ending. I dont know. My grandmother used to reminisce, my mother used to cry. All recent history is about death. When you look at photos taken in the late nineteenth century what occurs to you is that all of those people are dead. If you go back a bit further everyone is still dead but it doesnt matter. Those deaths are less to us. But the brown figures in the photographs are something else. Even their smiles are woeful. Filled with regret. With accusation.

You dont think this is just your own maudlin view?

No.

Wasnt your father seen by the family as the villain in this drama?

Yes. Of course. My grandmother was horrified when my mother went to work at Y-12. She didnt know what it was about but she thought the chances of it being something good were pretty much zero. But those werent just the best paying jobs within five hundred miles. They were the only paying jobs. My mother was fresh out of high school and working as a waitress at a drive-in. She was really smart and she should have been in college but there wasnt any money. She'd expected to get a scholarship out of the State beauty contest but she came in third. Which was something of an embarrassment because everyone knew the fix was in. She felt sorry for the winner because of the lame congratulations and she tried to be her friend but that didnt really work out. She was a straight A student and valedictorian of her class but she wound up third runner-up in the Miss Tennessee contest. Just out of the scholarship money. So that was that. She told me that the Tennessee Eastman employment office was in a plywood shack and that when she got there in the dark at five oclock in the morning the line was already the length of a football field and the mud was ankle deep. But she had the job.

What did she do?

She was a calutron girl.

What's a calutron?

How much do you want to know?

I dont know. Whatever you think.

All right. To build a uranium bomb you first have to separate the U-238 found in nature from U-235. In a thousand pounds of natural uranium there's only about seven pounds of U-235, so that's a lot of shoveling just to get started. There are several ways of separating it—enriching it, they like to say—and the electromagnetic system isnt the best, it was just the first. The calutron was invented by E O Lawrence and it was basically a mass spectrometer and acted as the collection device for the enriched uranium. Cal was short for California. Tron is just from the Greek. A measuring scale, or maybe an instrument. The uranium was first combined with chlorine and the resulting uranium tetrachloride was then ionized and driven by a series of electromagnets around what they called the racetrack. The racetrack was over a hundred feet long and the magnets were twenty feet tall. You have to think big. Because of the war they couldnt find enough copper to make the coils for the magnets, the conductors, so they went to the US Treasury Department and borrowed fourteen thousand tons of silver and trucked that in and used it.

Borrowed.

Borrowed. They returned it after the war. The first tracks they designed, the Alpha tracks, werent all that efficient so they took the material it produced and ran it again through a new design called the Beta and it actually came out weapons grade. In reality the Beta was not all that different. It was even smaller—about half the size of the Alpha, with ten foot magnets. The calutrons themselves were inserted into the racetracks sideways and the collectors were removed periodically and emptied. Of course what made the whole system workable was that U-238 is three neutrons heavier than U-235 so that it follows a greater arc in a magnetic field.

Of course.

Jesus.

Sorry. Please continue.

You sure?

Yes. Please.

There were eventually nine huge brick buildings that housed all of this. They may still be there for all I know. They looked like enormous shoe factories. Five Alpha tracks and four Beta. Eleven hundred and fifty-two calutrons in all. They ran continually and each girl monitored a single calutron. There was no talking. The girls sat on stools in long hallways and monitored the dials and adjusted the knobs so as to keep the beamcurrent maximized. It was a slow process. The U-235 for the Little Boy bomb that leveled Hiroshima was carried to Santa Fe on the train a few pounds at a time in a briefcase by an army officer in a business suit. When they had sixty-four kilos they were good.

He wouldnt become radiated? The chap in the suit.

No.

Could you explain topology in something like that straightforward a manner?

You're not being facetious?

No. I'm not.

I dont think so. The electromagnetic separation process is a very simple mechanical operation. You could explain it to a ten year old. Topology is about the mathematics of shapes. I could say that Poincaré's conjecture has to do with the inherently spherical nature of shapes that appear to be otherwise. Almost. But that may not even be a good example. Particularly if the conjecture is wrong. Well. For Poincaré it wasnt even a conjecture. It was more a query.

Do you think it's wrong?

No. But that may be hard to prove.

And your father was on an inspection tour of Y-12 and saw your mother.

Yes. He slipped her a note.

To call him.

Yes.

Did she?

No. He came back two days later and handed her a piece of note-paper and a pencil and she looked at it a minute and then wrote down her number. And her name. It was just the number of the hall phone in the dormitory. But the next day he called her.

And.

And here I am.

Lawrence was the man who invented the cyclotron.

Yes. He used to come to Y-12 and sit down and crank up the gain on one of the calutrons and show everybody how much more it was capable of producing and then get up and leave. In about five minutes the whole thing would be on fire. My father said that when Lawrence was working on the cyclotron at Berkeley he would pull this big copper switch and it was like a Frankenstein movie. Sheets of flame would leap across the lab and then the entire campus would go dark. They referred to Oak Ridge as Dogpatch. After the Li'l Abner cartoon. Toward the end of the war the gaseous diffusion plant at K-25 was up and running and they shut down the Alpha tracks but they still ran everything from K-25 through the Beta machines.

How long did your mother do this?

Two years. A little less.

How old was she when she met your father?

Nineteen. I think. Maybe twenty.

And he was?

Early thirties. I'm not even sure exactly when he was born. He wasnt very forthcoming about his early life. He'd been married before. Bobby found out about it.

Did your mother know this?

No. He knew that she wouldnt marry him if she knew.

He had no children by his first marriage.

He had a little boy. Who died of polio when he was about four. I think about him.

You think about him?

Yes. He was my brother.

When did your parents divorce?

I went to see her. She wasnt very happy about it.

I'm sorry?

I went to see her. His first wife. She was living in California.

Was she surprised to see you?

I dont think so. She'd heard rumors about me and she figured I'd show up sooner or later.

This was after your father died.

Yes.

What did she say?

She said: Well. You turned out all right. She was pretty dishy herself.

What else?

Not much. She said what was the point. My brother's name was Aaron.

She was Jewish.

Yes.

He had a predilection for Jewish women. Your father.

He didnt know my mother was Jewish.

Was she a physicist? His first wife.

No. She was a medical doctor. A cardiologist. But she worked in a lab. I dont know why my father divorced.

Twice.

Twice. Yes. It wasnt their idea.

The wives.

The wives. Yes.

Can I ask if he was a philanderer?

I dont know. I dont know that he wasnt. Did you get cigarettes?

Yes. They're in my case. Somewhere. Here.

Thank you.

I brought a lighter but I didnt think about an ashtray.

I can use the glass.

All right. Did your parents fight?

No. Toward the end he wasnt around all that much. He spent a lot of time in the South Pacific blowing things up.

That sounds pretty much a criticism.

It's not a criticism. Boys like blowing things up.

You're serious.

Yes.

How old were you when they separated?

I dont know. I think it was sort of gradual.

What else happened? Neither ever remarried.

No. I think they loved each other. It just became more and more difficult. She looks nervous. She's smoking faster. Of course this could be a false tell. She's a devious little bitch.

Me again I suppose. A false tell.

It's not important. What the else was that happened was that my mother had what was then called a nervous breakdown.

A nervous breakdown.

In the parlance of the times. She was hospitalized. A couple of times. We went to live with my grandmother. It was never discussed.

How old were you?

Four. When I started grammar school at St Mary's in Knoxville I wasnt six yet. I was at the head of my class by the end of the first week and that shut them all up.

If it was never discussed how did you know what was going on?

It wasnt hard to put it together. I remember my mother lying unconscious on the diningroom floor and I didnt know what to do but Bobby started crying so I started crying too, even though I wasnt sure how I felt about it.

Bobby started crying?

Yes.

How old was he?

He would have been ten.

This was in Los Alamos.

Yes.

What do you think was the nature of her emotional problems?

I dont know. After she was diagnosed with cancer the other symptoms went away. Then she died.

Did you ever ask her?

Once. She denied everything. Pretty much.

I would think it would be hard to deny.

How long have you been in this business did you say?

All right. Did you talk to your brother about it?

Yes.

What did he say?

He said that she'd had a nervous breakdown. I suppose you're seeking a genetic disposition to an unspecified and possibly nonexistent illness.

Maybe I just want to get a sense of how you feel about your family.

Where can I put this?

You've only taken a few puffs.

I know.

Let me have it. It strikes me that these aberrant experiences of yours commenced about the time your mother died. Were you very close?

We got along okay. But she listened to the doctors and she went to her grave thinking her daughter was crazy.

Was that painful for you?

Yes. It was. Worse after she died. I could see what her life had been and I felt bad about it. I needed my grandmother and I didnt really take into consideration that as for myself I was not what she needed at all. I didnt take into consideration the fact that she had just lost her daughter. A short time after that I had a dream about her. My mother. She was dead in the dream and she was being carried through the streets in a boat on the shoulders of a crowd. The boat was heaped with flowers and there was music. Almost like band music. Trumpets. When the cortege came around the corner I could see her face pale as a mask among the flowers. And when it came down the street past me. And then they passed on. And then I woke up.

Do you know what the dream was about?

No.

Are you okay?

Yes. I'm okay.

You never had the dream again.

No.

Do you have recurring dreams?

Yes. I suppose that sometimes the unconscious will keep working on certain dreams, revising them, hoping you'll get it. That's not the interesting part though.

What's the interesting part?

The interesting part is that it knows that you havent gotten it. It doesnt really have anything to go on. It's a mind reader? Sometimes it will just keep trying the same story over and over. It's stuck. It has no place to go. The recurring dream I've had is also pretty unusual—unheard of, really—in that the dreamer is not in it.

Are you in every dream you have?

Yes.

You think people dont have dreams that they're not in.

People are interested in other people. But your unconscious is not. Or only as they might directly affect you. It's been hired to do a very specific job. It never sleeps. It's more faithful than God.

What was the dream?

Why should I tell you?

You're kidding.

Maybe. Maybe not.

Have you ever told anyone?

No.

So you and I would be the only ones who knew this subliminal story.

You've been so sweet since the baby came.

I'm sorry?

Sorry. It's an expression of a friend of my brother's. I'm not even sure what it means. It's all right. The dream doesnt hold some secret concerning me. Or I dont think it does. It's just a dream. Fateful words. It's more like an old fable. Or perhaps even an old history. Repeated ad something.

But you're not in it.

No. Although I may be the dreamer generations hence who is piecing together some reconstruction by her elder's side at the fire.

Do you believe in a collective unconscious?

I'd be more likely to credit a thing like that if it hadnt become the property of Dr Jung.

Maybe we should get to the dream.

I havent said I'd tell you.

You know you're going to.

Okay. The women look up from their washing and they understand at once that everything they have loved and nurtured has been put at naught. They have in an instant no past and no future. Everything they've taught their children has been stricken from the world without a trace and they are now widows and slaves. What they've seen is a mounted army gathered out of nowhere that stands aligned upon the hills above the village. The riders are clothed in skins and their horses wear shields of rawhide painted with circular geometries pale with dust. The men of the village have come from the huts with axe and spear but they will soon lie in pools of their communal blood and the women will be raped and the village torched and burned and they will then march weeping and bleeding and yoked like livestock to a country they've never seen, never imagined.

This seems very elaborate for a dream.

You come to know it in more detail with repetition.

So what do you think it means?

I dont know what it means. I've always thought that one of the women was my mother.

But you yourself are no part of it.

No.

What else?

Unless of course I'm inside my mother. Hadnt thought of that. What else? I dont know. I've never told the dream to anyone before.

Do you think it's related to something you've read?

When was the last time you dreamt about something you'd read?

You dont think that happens.

No. Do you?

I dont know. I'd have to think about it. Do you remember the first time that they took you to the doctor's?

For being crazy?

Okay.

Yes. They took me to Knoxville. I was four.

Crazy at four.

An aggravated case. They took me to the eye doctor. I had strabismus.

They didnt take you to the eye doctor for being crazy.

No. It was the eye doctor who told them that I was. They thought I was weird but it had never occurred to them to take me to a doctor about it. Maybe they were afraid they wouldnt get me back. Or that they would. Anyway, that was the beginning of my life among the shrinks.

What do you remember about that day?

Such as what?

Just in general.

Just in general.

Yes.

All right. I got up around seven and went downstairs and my grandmother was in the kitchen and she gave me a glass of orange juice and then she told me to go up and wake my mother.

How did you know that it was seven oclock?

I looked at the kitchen clock.

You could tell time.

Yes.

At four.

Yes.

Go on.

I was in my pajamas with the dogs on them and I went up and woke my mother and she asked me what time it was and I told her and then I went back down to the kitchen and Granellen put me in my chair.

Your grandmother.

Yes. She was fixing breakfast and the radio was on and I could see out the window. I could see Granellen's car parked in the driveway. The car was blue and she'd just gotten it. I think it was only the second car she ever had. It was wintertime and there was a fire in the stove and the trees outside were bare and the cows had come up to the fence at the bottom of the drive and the trees along the creek were gray and dead-looking. I had a bowl of cornflakes and my mother came down and had some coffee and then she took me upstairs and got me dressed. I wore my green corduroy skirt with the shoulderstraps and a green sweater and my Poll Parrot shoes with the straps that snapped. We left for Knoxville a little before eight oclock.

Okay. I think I get it. Why dont you just tell me what the doctor said.

He said Hi what's your name?

This is the optometrist.

Ophthalmologist. And I thought that this was peculiar because after all we didnt just wander in off the street. My mother had called and made an appointment. So I knew that the whole thing was completely bogus from the get-go but I told him my name and I asked him who it was that he was expecting.

What did he say?

He didnt say anything. People dont listen to four year olds. He looked at my mother and smiled but it was a fishy sort of a smile and I was wishing I could just get the hell out of there.

You thought that he should know who you were because your mother had made an appointment with him.

Yes.

And he thought there was something unusual about you.

Well. The conversation sort of deteriorated. But yes. He thought there was something wrong with me.

Was that the first time you had had a sense of that?

No. It was just the first time anyone told my mother.

What did he tell her?

I dont know. Nothing good.

Did your mother say anything about it?

She said that I was rude to the doctor. After we got in the car. She used to tell me that I needed to have my head examined. But it was just a sort of family expression. What it really meant was that I dont agree with you. But now she said that we were going to. Get it examined. She was upset.

Because of your rudeness to the doctor?

She thought he actually knew what he was talking about. I dont know why. He was a bloody ophthalmologist. But when we left I could see that she was worried. About herself mostly, I suppose. I suppose she could see herself saddled with a child who was both blind and crazy.

You thought all this?

I thought most of it. You reflect with an older mind. But the ideas are still there. Memory has substance. It's not nothing.

She took you to a psychiatrist.

A psychologist actually.

And what happened?

Nothing happened. I was four years old. Hard to diagnose mental disorders in four year olds.

Was this a difficult time for you?

No. Just for them. I loved my grandmother. I used to sit in the kitchen in the morning while she made biscuits. She would roll them out with a marble rollingpin and I would sit there and draw and color. I loved the winters. There would be snow on the ground and a fire in the stove.

Where was your father all this time?

My father was in the South Pacific blowing things up.

You were diagnosed as autistic by more than one analyst. Before it was well understood. Well, before it was understood at all. Because of course it's still not understood.

Sure. If you have a patient with a condition that's not understood why not ascribe it to a disorder that is also not understood? Autism occurs in males more than it does in females. So does higher order mathematical intuition. We think: What is this about? Dont know. What is at the heart of it? Dont know. All I can tell you is that I like numbers. I like their shapes and their colors and their smells and the way they taste. And I dont like to take people's word for things. My father finally did stay with us during the last months of my mother's illness. He had a study in the smokehouse out back. He'd cut a big square hole in the wall and put in a window so he could look out at the fields and the creek beyond. His desk was a wooden door set up on sawhorses and there was an old leather sofa there that was stuffed with horsehair. It was all dried and cracked and the horsehair was leaking out but he put a blanket over it. I went in one day and sat at his

desk and looked at the problem he was working on. I already knew
some math. Quite a bit, actually. I tried to puzzle out the paper
but it was hard. I loved the equations. I loved the big sigma signs
with the codes for the summations. I loved the narrative that was
unfolding. My father came in and found me there and I thought
I was in trouble and I jumped up but he took me by the hand
and led me back to the chair and sat me down and went over the
paper with me. His explanations were clear. Simple. But it was
more than that. They were filled with metaphor. He drew a couple
of Feynman diagrams and I thought they were pretty cool. They
mapped the world of the subatomic particles he was attempting
to explain. The collisions. The weighted routes. I understood—
really understood—that the equations were not a supposition of
the form whose life was confined to the symbols on the page which
described them but that they were there before my eyes. In actual-
ity. They were in the paper, the ink, in me. The universe. Their
invisibility could never speak against them or their being. Their
age. Which was the age of reality itself. Which was itself invisible
and always had been. He never let go of my hand.

Are you all right?

Yes. I'm sorry.

Do you want another cigarette?

No. I dont even like them. Let's stop.

All right. Can I ask you something?

Sure.

What about just some memory of your brother.

My brother.

Yes.

Oh boy. All right. The beach house in North Carolina. When I
got up in the morning and went to his room he'd already gone out
and I fixed a thermos of tea and went down to the beach in the dark
and he was sitting there in the sand and we had tea and waited for
the sun. We watched through our dark glasses as it came red and

dripping up out of the sea. We'd walked on the beach the night before and there was a moon and a mock moon that rode in the rings and we talked about the paraselene and I said something to the effect that to speak of such things which are composed solely of light as problematic or perhaps as wrongly seen or even wrongly known or of questionable reality had always seemed to me something of a betrayal. He looked at me and he said betrayal? And I said yes. Things composed of light. In need of our protection. Then in the morning we sat in the sand and drank our tea and watched the sun come up.

IV

Good morning.

Good morning.

How are things going? You seem a bit somber.

Somber.

Do you have everything you need?

Could you be more specific?

Sorry. I guess I'm just asking if you're reasonably comfortable. If there's anything I can do for you.

Why dont we just get started.

I'm not just being polite.

All right. How about a pingpong net?

Do you play pingpong?

No.

The general rule is to try to minimize any possible opportunity for the patients to harm themselves. So you really have to be pretty scrupulous. No belts or ropes or anything like that. Glass, sharp objects.

Ergo stainless steel mirrors.

Yes.

Have you been finding a lot of patients dangling from pingpong nets?

No, but it's probably happened. Somewhere. How about something I might put in a request for without making a lot of trouble.

No deal. It's nets or nothing.

Sorry. What should we talk about?

I dont know. Ask me three questions and then I'll ask you three.

Okay.

Okay?

Sure.

Who goes first?

You can go first.

All right. Anything?

I think so.

Okay. What's your wife's name?

Edwina.

You're kidding me. Oh shit. I'm sorry. I shouldnt have said that.

It's all right.

Does she have a nickname?

Ed.

You call your wife Ed?

Yes. That's three questions.

Come on.

All right. One more.

How long have you been married?

Eleven years. Altogether. After we divorced I was a bachelor for three years. Then we remarried and we've been married ever since. How many questions is that?

Why did you get divorced?

You asked me that.

I know. Were you bad?

That's a bit personal.

Were you?

That's it. My turn.

You didnt answer. Do you take your wife out?

Yes. Of course.

Where do you go?

We go to dinner. Sometimes with friends. We go to movies. We're members of the Symphony. We go bowling.

You dont go bowling.

No. It must be my turn.

All right. Fire away.

It was just a joke. The bowling.

Bowling is not a joke. I love bowling. Bowling is my life.

I dont think so. Do you keep a diary?

No.

You've never kept a diary?

I didnt say I'd never kept one.

But not lately.

Not lately. Have you ever read a patient's diary?

No.

I would think it might be useful.

You just want to know if I'm honest. How old were you when you learned to read?

Four.

Did your mother teach you?

Not exactly. I learned by looking on with her while she read to me at bedtime. When she found out that I could read it scared her. But it was your fault, right?

The divorce.

Yes.

Yes. It was.

And then she took you back. After three years.

Yes. Mercifully.

Did you beg on your knees?

No. I think it's my turn.

But some pretty dedicated courting, right?

Yes.

Okay.

You dont have any friends. Does this mean you find people boring?

No. People surprise me all the time.

Do I surprise you?

I think you asked me that. Let's just say you dont startle me.

Have you been seeing anyone?

Jesus. Seeing?

Yes.

I dont see people.

Never.

No.

I take this to be a conscious decision on your part. Can I ask how you came by it?

Ask away. I'm your creature.

I dont think so.

The man I wanted wouldnt have me. So that was that. I couldnt stop loving him. So my life was pretty much over.

The mystery man.

Yes.

It could hardly be someone I know. Is it someone I know of?

I'd prefer not to say.

Still, you must have had suitors.

Quaint, that. Suitors. Would that include drunken hayseeds try-ing to feel you up on the dance floor?

I dont think so. You look uncomfortable.

Beyond my normal look?

I think so. The man you were in love with. How long ago was this?

Am in love with.

Am, then.

Probably we should drop it.

All right.

I havent had as much interest as you might think. I've had to accept the fact that I'm a bit scary. Plus the onus of lunacy of course. Why do I have the feeling you're not going to leave this alone?

Sorry. I guess I should say that I'm surprised to hear you describe yourself as a lunatic.

I didnt say that I so described myself. Still if I insist that I'm sane you have to consider the source of the claim. And of course it shouldnt come as a surprise to find that people in rubber rooms have a worldview at odds with that of the people who put them there.

You're not claiming equal legitimacy for the two views.

Okay.

Okay what?

Not if it would be a problem for you.

I feel we keep drifting away from the subject.

Which is?

You.

Well.

I think the sense of being an alien—as distinct from merely feeling alienated—is fairly common among mental patients.

Or among aliens.

There's a classic trope in which the killer catches a glimpse of himself in a mirror. He suddenly sees a crazed figure spattered with blood holding an axe aloft and he realizes that it is he himself he is looking at. In the story it usually suggests a link to a buried conscience. How would you interpret this? What is being revealed?

A taste for melodrama? Let me ask you something.

Okay.

Why do you let me bully you?

I dont know. Do I?

It's not important. The world you live in is shored up by a collective of agreements. Is that something you think about? The hope is that the truth of the world somehow lies in the common experience of it. Of course the history of science and mathematics and even philosophy is a good bit at odds with this notion. Innovation and discovery by definition war against the common understanding. One should be wary. What do you think?

I dont know. I'm not sure what your view is.

I dont have a view. I used to. Now I dont. Although I have to say—again—that solipsism has always seemed to me a fairly inarguable position.

Would you reconsider medication? I'm sure that there are options you havent considered.

You're digging a dry hole.

You've never really articulated your objections.

To your satisfaction.

If you like.

You dont know what antipsychotics are and you dont know how they work. Or why. All we have finally is the spectacle of tardive dyskinetics feeling their way along the wall. Jerking and drooling and muttering. Of course for those trekking toward the void there are waystations where the news will very suddenly become altogether bleaker. Maybe a sudden chill. There's data in the world available only to those who have reached a certain level of wretchedness. You dont know what's down there if you havent been down there. Joy on the other hand hardly even teaches gratitude. A thoughtful silence.

Just a silence.

Its general vacuity aside there seems to be a ceiling to well-being. My guess is that you can only be so happy. While there seems to be no floor to sorrow. Each deeper misery being a state heretofore unimagined. Each suggestive of worse to come.

I seem to remember starting out on a somewhat cheerier note.

Sorry.

I wonder if you could put into words what most troubles you. For all our chats I still have little idea of your life.

Dont sweat it, Doctor. We're on our way to a wholly hypothetical world, we two. We'll be happier when we get there.

I'll have to take your word for it. Do you still play the violin?

No.

Were you playing it?

Sporadically.

You couldnt find time to practice.

Wouldnt.

How good did you think you would have to be?

At least in the top ten.

In the world?

Yes. In the world. Where else?

How did you know that you were as good at math as you were?

You just know. It's not even a question.

Do you think that music has a therapeutic effect?

I should hark myself back thereto?

It's just a question.

I suppose it depends on the music.

Power to soothe the savage beast.

Breast.

Excuse me?

Power to soothe the savage breast. And it's charms to soothe, actually.

Are you sure?

Jesus.

Sorry. Do you miss the violin?

Yes. Very much.

Do you think you might have a tendency to divest yourself of the things in your life that actually sustain you?

I suppose this is psychology. I dont know the answer to your question. What? Do I? Do we? How would such a predilection stack up against the world's own desire to divest one of just those things. I think I understand your question. We've been there before. And it may be a superstition with us that if we will just give up those things we are fond of then the world will not take from us what we truly love. Which of course is a folly. The world knows what you love.

Interesting.

I gave up apologizing for myself a long time ago. What should I say? That I'm sorry to be that which I am? I'd very little to do with it. As to your question—to concede to my taste for sweeping generalities—I might well say that what smacks of conundrum is usually just a thesis badly stated. Which I think I've suggested before. It's really just a rather bald rendering of Wittgenstein. I dont know. Maybe we could talk about something else.

I sort of like this.

Oh boy.

I'm just teasing. Who is Miss Vivian?

She was an older woman. Thin. Eccentric. She dressed garishly and wore slabs of makeup. A shabby fur stole. She would look at you through this rhinestone lorgnette and she smoked cigarettes in an ivory holder.

You speak of her in the past tense.

I havent seen her for a while.

Was she one of the Kid's acts?

No.

Did you talk to her?

Sure. We'd sit and chat. She was pretty unhappy. Her makeup would be streaked from crying. Or gullied, in her case.

What was she unhappy about?

She was unhappy about the babies. She used to cry about the babies.

The babies?

Yes.

What babies?

I dont know. All of them I guess.

Why was this of particular interest to you?

Because I cried nonstop the first two years of my life.

Reason enough, I suppose. Did you know why she was crying about the babies?

She didnt say. Other than the fact that they were unhappy. Are you sure this is something you want to go into?

It's up to you. Yes. I would.

She was gone for a long time. And I was surprised to find that I missed her. I had a dream about her. I thought that the fact that I missed her and wanted to talk to her would make her come back. But it didnt. What was the dream?

Sorry?

I was just saying your next question for you.

All right. What was the dream.

It was a dream about children crying. When I woke up they were still crying. It just got farther away. I dont think that it had stopped. I just couldnt hear it anymore. I hadnt been around babies much. But I got to wondering why they cried all the time.

I think they cry for different reasons. Dont they? They're wet, or they're hungry.

I thought there had to be more to it. Animals might whimper if they're hungry or cold. But they dont start screaming. It's a bad idea. The more noise you make the more likely you are to be eaten. If you've no way to escape you keep silent. If birds couldnt fly they wouldnt sing. When you're defenseless you keep your opinions to yourself.

That sounds metaphorical.

It's just biology.

All right.

What was startling was the anguish in those cries. I began paying attention. There were always babies at the bus station and they were always crying. And these were not mild complaints. I couldnt understand how the least discomfort could take the form of agony.

No other creature was so sensitive. The more I thought about it the clearer it became to me that what I was hearing was rage. And the most extraordinary thing was that no one seemed to find this extraordinary. Except for Miss Vivian. Of course you could point out that however gracious or kind or concerned she might be she was still an old looney. Of problematic reality. So I took that home with me. I dont think we ever really discussed it. She would just start weeping and shaking her head. I thought if she had brought me all this baggage she must be expecting me to do something about it but it began to get more complicated. I thought about it. The rage of children seemed inexplicable other than as a breach of some deep and innate covenant having to do with how the world should be and wasnt. I understood that their raw exposure to the world was the world.

You dont think this is all a bit fanciful?

I do think.

How would a child know how the world should be?

A child would have to be born so. A sense of justice is common to the world. All mammals certainly. A dog knows perfectly well what is fair and what is not. He didnt learn it. He came with it. Would you like to get more fanciful?

In for a penny.

More fanciful would be the understanding that the idea of justice and the idea of the human soul are two forms of the same consideration.

You didnt just come up with that.

No.

What about the animals?

They're not screaming. Of course fanciful may itself be code for deranged. Anyway, this led pretty directly to the next question.

Which is?

At what age in a child's life does rage become sorrow?

I dont know. I dont think Piaget addresses the question. Or why.

I think I know why. The injustice over which they are so distraught is irremediable. And rage is only for what you believe can be fixed. All the rest is grief. At some point they get this.

I think that an innate sense of justice might be a difficult concept to sell. That children could have this sense at birth.

They have little else. A fear of falling. Loud noises. A love of the breast. Everything else is potential. The schema is there but nothing has arrived. Things which are innate and well formed are rare. And primitive. And necessary. When you hear a sobbing child say it's not fair you are always hearing the truth.

And Miss—is it Vivian?

Vivian.

Miss Vivian. Was sent to tell you this.

I dont know. I always suspected that it was just a thing I had to understand before we could move on to the next issue.

What is the next issue?

That's not so easy. I dont claim to have a very good handle on it. If you said that the world itself contains the antidote to all that is troubling about it I would say that wasnt entirely wrong. But funding this is the notion that there is an order to the world not predicated upon the endless problematic of addressing its most recent iteration.

I'm not sure I understand that. It sounds somewhat platonic.

I know. But the suggestion is not that there is a reality of which perception is just a shadow but that there is a reality that is durable enough to support its own endless experimentation.

You arrived here with a toothbrush. Why is that? Well. Plus the cash of course.

I dont know. My life has always been pretty austere. Bobby used to take me shopping and then the clothes would just hang in the closet. I suppose I had a hard time giving up the Amati.

Have you given it up?

I dont know. I would still like to play. It's always there. The first time I heard Bach I had an out-of-body experience. I was maybe ten. I remember watching myself sitting on the sofa in the livingroom. Listening. I didnt even think it was odd.

Have you had other out-of-body experiences?

Not from music. But that one time changed me. It was as if a key had turned. It was physical. I was never the same person again.

If not from music what?

I got stung by wasps once and I ran into the kitchen and then I saw Granellen come in and bend down over me. I was lying on the floor and I could see myself lying there looking down. I wondered if I was going to die but just in a vague sort of way. Granellen put some ice wrapped in a towel on my face and after a while I sat up.

Someone once said that the raw material of art is pain. Is that true of music?

I dont know. I've never composed music. But I would guess it might be true.

What about mathematics?

Mathematics is just sweat and toil. I wish it were romantic. It isnt. At its worst there are audible suggestions. It's hard to keep up. You dont dare sleep and you may have been up for two days but that's too bad. You find yourself making a decision and finding two more decisions waiting and then four and then eight. You have to force yourself to just stop and go back. Begin again. You're not seeking beauty, you're seeking simplicity. The beauty comes later. After you've made a wreck of yourself.

Is it worth it?

Like nothing else on earth.

What do you think is the one indispensable gift?

Faith.

This is a rather animated you.

Well. You tricked me.

You think that it must be different from music. Math.

The rules of music that guide a composer like Bach . . . All right. There are not any composers like Bach. There's just Bach. But ignoring that for the moment, these rules can be learned by laymen. They are there to be learned. Or not. They are there whether the first note of music was ever written or not. Is that true?

It sounds like platonic music. To me.

Yes. It's at least that bad. Schopenhauer thought that if the universe vanished music alone would remain. The rules are the music. Without the rules you have nothing but noise. When we hear a wrong note we wince. We smile or weep or march to war. Can you explain any of that? How do you know when someone is dancing? What if they are dancing out of time with the music?

I dont know.

No. But this set of rules—I think I'd call them laws, laws of music—is selfcontained and complete. They are known and there will never be any more of them. Is that true of mathematics? Is there such a thing as a grand unifying theory of mathematics? Hilbert's second thesis? Cantor's dream? It seems more than unlikely. Langlands or no. And yet must there not be at least a description of mathematics? Both as it is and as it is to become? I wanted to do mathematics. But I wanted to understand it as well. And I never would. I couldnt even frame the question.

I'm surprised to hear you say that understanding mathematics was beyond you. Is this something that concerns most mathematicians? Or do they just go about the business of computation?

I think for most it's a passing concern. At best.

You said that mathematics was mostly hard work. But I'm still not sure how you go about it.

Yes. The first thing you do is take off your shoes and socks. To have a parallel access to the base ten.

How do you know I wont believe you?

How do you know you shouldnt? The core question is not how you do math but how does the unconscious do it. How is it that it's demonstrably better at it than you are? You work on a problem and then you put it away for a while. But it doesnt go away. It reappears at lunch. Or while you're taking a shower. It says: Take a look at this. What do you think? Then you wonder why the shower is cold. Or the soup. Is this doing math? I'm afraid it is. How is it doing it? We dont know. I've posed the question to some pretty good mathematicians. How does the unconscious do math? Some who'd thought about it and some who hadnt. For the most part they seemed to think it unlikely that the unconscious went about it the same way we did. What was surprising to me was the insouciance with which they greeted this news. As if the very nature of mathematics had not just been hauled into the dock. A few thought that if it had a better way of doing mathematics it ought to tell us about it. Well, maybe. Or maybe it thinks we're not smart enough to understand it.

I'm not sure I see how that would work.

Neither does anybody else. Sometimes you get a clear sense that doing math is largely just feeding data into the substation and waiting to see what comes out. I'm not even sure that it's all that wise to commit things to memory. What you log in becomes fixed. In a way that the machinations of the unconscious would appear not to. I dont really like to write things down. Is that good? I dont know. Grothendieck writes everything down. Witten nothing. But I think for most people to leave things unrecorded is to leave them free to look around for fresh analogies. They go about their business and come back from time to time and report to you. A written statement—or an equation—is a sort of signpost. A waystation. It tells you where you are and gives you a new place to start from. Dirac draws pictures. I dont think he believes there exist graphic representations of entities too small to subtend a particle of light, but he has an engineering background and it's stuck with him. Odd things come in handy. People who are good with an abacus can calculate pretty well with an imaginary one.

Is that true?

No. I made it up. Jesus.

Sorry. I'm not sure I've heard a description of the unconscious that grants it that kind of autonomy.

Well. It's been on its own for a long time. Of course it has no access to the world except through your own sensorium. Otherwise it would just labor in the dark. Like your liver. For historical reasons it's loath to speak to you. It prefers drama, metaphor, pictures. But it understands you very well. And it has no other cause save yours.

Do we have a working relationship with the unconscious? Is it a reciprocal arrangement?

No. That would be a stretch.

Are you free to ignore it?

Sure. If you like. You might call that manual override. Not always such a good idea of course.

Have you talked to other therapists about these ideas?

Not much. They bore pretty easily.

What did they say? If they didnt get too bored.

Nothing. They'd write it down. Or write something down. Or I'd change the subject.

Like now.

No. We're still okay.

I suppose your reservations about the souldoctors have a long history.

Fair to say.

What is your biggest complaint?

I dont know. Maybe their lack of imagination. Their confusion about the categories into which they're given to sorting their patients. As if name and cure were one. The way they ignore the total lack of evidence for the least efficacy in their treatments. Other than that they're fine.

That's reassuring.

Anyway, it's a nice little cottage industry you've cobbled up for yourselves. The subject at hand would seem to be reality and that in itself is pretty funny. Still, you probably get up to a minimum of mischief. If you serve to keep the patients clothed and fed and off the street that's a good thing.

The Kid. Does he attempt to influence you? Does he tell you what to do? I asked you this before but I'm not clear on it.

I'll have to get back to you.

I'm sorry?

I'll have to think up another answer. I'm sure he's advised me on what I should do. From time to time. As for influencing me, why else would he be there?

Do you think a voice can compel a person to commit suicide?

You suspect that the Kid has been quietly moving yours truly to the edge?

It's just a question.

If a person has auditory hallucinations she's going to have some definable relationship with the voice. Most suicides dont need a voice. What should give you pause is that suicide scales with intelligence in the animal kingdom and you might wonder if this is not true of individuals as well as of species. I would.

Do you think that there is something suicides have in common? Some common mindset?

Yes. They dont like it here.

Well.

I'm being a smartass. I'm not in the best of moods. Which I'm sure you've picked up on.

Do you want to stop?

I'm okay.

All right.

I suppose if the world is your construct then to discuss it in terms of its own autonomy is going to be an uncertain business. It's a perception, and as such I'm not sure what it would mean for it to have its own life. I would say that it doesnt. It has your life. And then it doesnt.

This is something you've said before.

I suppose.

To other counselors.

Yes.

How did they respond?

They didnt.

And what would you do?

I dont know. I've broken out laughing on occasion.

But you were serious in what you said.

Yes.

And what would they do then?

You know what they would do.

Write it down.

Yes.

What would they write?

Who knows? Patient possibly hebephrenic. Anyway, all of this became less of a concern. I couldnt take them seriously.

What made it less of a concern?

Greater concerns.

I never know how seriously to take remarks like that.

I know.

When you were on antipsychotics the visitations stopped.

The visitations.

Yes.

It sounds like a religious experience.

Sorry.

That a drug can restructure the world into something like an objective reality is a claim with as little validity as the objective reality itself. I think what I said at the time was that I had no more reason to place my confidence in a drugged state of mind than in a sober one.

You wouldnt be willing to try another medication.

You asked me that.

All right. If someone were to come into the room while the Kid was there might they see him?

And that. But probably not.

But not exclusively not.

I dont know.

If they were on the reality drug with the rest of us then I suppose not.

I suppose.

Do you want to take a break?

Sure. How about a smoke?

Why not.

You dont carry those around with you.

No.

You keep them in the bottom drawer. So that nobody will carry them off?

So far so good.

Thank you. Did you bring an ashtray?

Yes. You could take those with you if you like.

That's all right. I'm not much of a smoker.

It's relaxing?

I dont know. Maybe it's being bad.

Really?

Sure.

How old were you when you first smoked a cigarette?

Three.

That's not true.

No. But not that much older. I stole a cigarette from my uncle's pack on the coffeetable and took a match from the kitchen and went out to the smokehouse and lit up. I was probably six.

Did you get sick?

What I remember was my head swimming. Still, I thought that if grown-ups did this there must be a reason for it.

I'm guessing that was a view with a limited shelflife.

I dont think most children seriously consider the fact that they are going to be adults one day. And that this is what they'll look like.

Did you?

Yes.

And?

I didnt see any way out of it.

When did you first think that suicide might be an option for you?

Think seriously?

Think seriously.

Maybe I'm not even sure what that means. When I was younger—ten, eleven—I had a sort of waking dream that was frightening to me. And then I realized that it was neither waking nor a dream. It was something else. And I had no reason to believe that what I saw did not exist and that if that realm was unknown to us that didnt make it less threatening but more.

What was the dream? Or the vision or whatever it was.

I saw through something like a judas hole into this world where there were sentinels standing at a gate and I knew that beyond the gate was something terrible and that it had power over me.

Something terrible.

Yes. A being. A presence. And that the search for shelter and for a covenant among us was simply to elude this baleful thing of which we were in endless fear and yet of which we had no knowledge.

You were how old?

Ten. I think ten.

Did you have this vision again?

No. There was nothing else to see. The keepers at the gate saw me and they gestured among themselves and then all of that went dark and I never saw it again. I called it the Archatron.

The presence beyond the gate.

The presence beyond the gate.

And it was shrouded away.

Yes.

But nothing is changed.

Nothing is changed. I wish it were a dream and I could wake. I wish I could forget it but I cant. I wish I could be who I was before but I never will be.

What else?

That's all. Everyone knows that the act of suicide is always there. Not too many people choose it. Nietzsche says that it can get you through many a bad night. Just the idea. But it's only for a few. People are very attached to their lives.

But not everybody.

No.

Let me try another tack.

Watch the boom.

Have you ever had the sense that the Kid and his companions were assigned to you?

Assigned.

Yes.

By whom?

I dont know. Maybe this sorts somehow with the question of whether or not they might have other clients.

We might have to inquire of the clients. Put an ad in the personals.

Maybe it just strikes me that a figure as well delineated as you describe the Kid to be might come equipped with something like a portfolio. I've still no idea what you make of him. The brain must have to use a good deal of energy to put together such a construct.

Not to mention maintaining it consistently over a period of years. What do you think could be worth such an outlay?

I dont know. It's a bitch, aint it?

Well. Something like that.

For me to be having this conversation with you—any conversation, I suppose—I have to make a series of concessions not just to your point of view but to the actual form of the world seen from your place in it. I can do that. But the problem is that for you it is never a question of point of view. You're never troubled to find yourself discussing quite peculiar things in a fairly normal way. Maybe it's just the naivete that you bring to the table. You might say: Well, how else would you discuss them? But when the subject is chimeras arent you already on somewhat shaky ground? I've thought from early on that the Kid was there not to supply something but to keep something at bay. And in the meantime the whole business is subsumed under the rubric of a single reality which itself remains unaddressable. I wake in the night in my room and lie there listening to the quiet. You ask where they are. I dont know where they are. But they are not nowhere. Nowhere like nothing requires for its affirmation a witness which it cannot supply by its own definition. You'd be loath to grant these beings a will of their own, but if they were not possessed of something like autonomy in what sense could they then be said to exist? I've no power either to conjure them forth or send them packing. I dont speak for them or see to their hygiene or their wardrobe. I said that they were indistinguishable from living beings, but the truth is that their reality is if anything more striking. Not just the Kid but all of them. Their movements, their speech, the color and the fold of their clothes. There's nothing dreamlike about them. None of this is much help, is it? Well, people dont listen to loonies. Until they say something funny.

Do you think that I listen to you?

Your prototypical looney. You asked me that before.

What did you answer before?

Let me put this out.

Here.

Thank you. You do okay. To answer your question.

What is it that he's keeping at bay?

The Kid?

The Kid.

I dont think there's a simple answer to that. If the world itself is a horror then there is nothing to fix and the only thing you could be protected from would be the contemplation of it.

How would that be a help? I dont understand.

I'm sorry. But that's really all I have.

You wake and you know that they are somewhere. The beings. But your explanation seems a bit philosophical. If it is an explanation.

I know. You could just ask what it is that chimeras do on their day off.

Yes. You could. Is Berkeley still a part of your life?

Everything in my life is a part of my life. I dont have the luxury of forgetting things. I was probably eight or nine before I realized that things went away. When people said that they didnt remember I thought it meant that they just didnt want to talk about it. Where I live things dont go away. Everything that has happened is pretty much still here.

Isnt it just a matter of degree? We're all of us pretty much an assemblage of memories.

I know. It's an uncertain business. I suppose I trust my memory of events largely because of the evidence I have for my ability at memorization. Are they the same? The lines of a poem have no substance other, but the events of history—including your personal history—have no substance at all. Their materiality has vanished without a trace. My experience has been that people with poor memories are just as ready to be right as anyone else.

Your world must be getting a bit crowded by now.

It is. Not everything is welcome. You have to be careful what you let in. But I wouldnt change it. I'll never escape Plato. Or Kant. Wittgenstein I regard as something of a contemporary. A fellow student. Husserl I fell in love with. He was a mathematician, so I trusted him. He was professor at Freiburg and he took in a young student named Martin Heidegger and was his teacher and his mentor and then the Nazis came and they said that Husserl would have to be dismissed because he was a Jew and Heidegger said why yes, that was only right. And so Husserl cleared out his desk and went home and sat and wept and then he died and Heidegger took over his chair. So the question that we're left with I suppose is that if human decency does not represent something like the foundation of philosophical inquiry then what is its purpose? Wittgenstein agonized his whole life over the state of his soul. The question never seems to have occurred to Heidegger. How did I get to be the counselor?

I dont know. You might have been a good one.

Probably not. I think that I'd have told people I didnt want to hear about their boring daylives and let's just cut directly to the dreams.

Do we do that?

Cut to the dreams?

I dont know.

We should have talked more about dreams?

We is not over.

I suppose. But she's a cunning little bitch. Every other word a lie no doubt. What's the linguistic connection between devious and deviant? What time is lunch?

Noon I think. Let me ask you this. If you were rejected by this man why couldnt you just get on with your life? You were what? Twelve?

Yes. A twelve year old slut.

That seems unlikely.

I'm just saying that I was a horny girl.

You were sexually active?

No. Of course not. But there was something about myself that I hadnt accepted. Sometimes it takes a somewhat disorienting experience to wrench you from your slumbers.

I take it that there was such an experience.

There was.

Is this something that you would be willing to share?

It will sound trivial.

All right.

It was in the hallway at school between classes.

In high school.

Yes. This boy who was a senior stopped me and asked me to turn around. He was captain of the basketball team and was generally thought to be about the coolest guy in the school. And he had a paper and a ballpoint in his hand and he made this twirling motion with his finger and he said: Let me borrow your back. And this girl was standing there with him watching and I turned around and he put the paper on my back and wrote on it. I dont know what it was. Maybe he just signed it. I dont know. And maybe he knew what he was doing. I mean he could have just used the wall. Or a locker door. But I turned around and he wrote on my back and I closed my eyes. It was enormously sensual. I thought at first that it was just that shivery feeling like someone's fingers going up your back. But it was more than that. I felt that he was writing something to me. I could feel the girl watching me. She was suddenly curious. She was probably sixteen. When he'd finished he said thanks and I opened my eyes and they were gone down the hall.

And that was all?

That was all. Yes.

I'm not sure what it is that you're telling me.

I know.

You said that it was sensual.

Yes.

Was it sexual?

Yes. Very.

So what was the realization?

The realization was that I was hopelessly in love and had been for some time. That my life had been resolved. While I wasnt looking, so to speak. Not that uncommon.

And that was that.

And that was that.

You were twelve.

Yes.

But you wont tell me who it was.

No.

How did you know that it was love? You'll excuse the skepticism.

How can you not? I was only at peace in his company. If peace is the word. I knew that I would love him forever. In spite of the laws of Heaven. And that I would never love anyone else.

And this has turned out to be the case.

Yes. It has.

But he didnt love you.

He loved me very much.

Well. I dont understand.

I know.

It must have been the age difference. That's the only thing I can think of.

I never saw that as a problem. I thought we could wait a year if it would make him more comfortable. Or two years even.

But still not enough to keep him out of jail.

The following summer we saw a great deal of each other. And the next summer.

You were thirteen.

By then I was fourteen. I thought that if I offered myself to him body and soul that he would take me without reservation. And he didnt.

No.

So where do you go with that? What would you wish for yourself?

I dont suppose there could be anything like a second choice.

Not unless you're suggesting death.

I'm not.

I know you're reluctant to acknowledge that this particular case might be hard to dismiss as a schoolgirl crush. I've always asked for special privileges and exemptions. Some things I didnt get just because I couldnt find anyone to explain them to. But a deprivation that demands you choose to dismiss either your past or your future is more than difficult. So I'm asking where would you begin again? As you suggest. Or how. Or more to the point, why?

You're not given pause by the fact that the overwhelming majority of people find a way to deal with their disappointments?

No.

That would be an exemption that you would claim.

Yes.

This conversation is beginning to take a fairly odd turn.

I know. A disappointed longing has a legacy of which its fulfillment can only dream.

The laws of Heaven. Would you want to elaborate on that?

No.

All right. Can we talk about your father? Again.

If you like.

But with no great enthusiasm.

It's all right. Go ahead.

You said that you didnt hold your father accountable.

I dont. For what it's worth. History will swallow them all up, along with their accountability. But the bomb is forever.

Where is Trinity? Is that in Nevada?

New Mexico.

Was your father there?

Yes. Of course.

Did he talk about that?

Not much. I've read the standard accounts. My father's group was about six miles from ground zero. They'd been given glasses that were very dark. I think something like welding goggles. But my father had brought his own because he didnt think you'd be able to see much with the government issue glasses. I guess you can read that as a metaphor. But all the glasses had to do was block the ultraviolet light. They listened to the countdown over a loudspeaker. They were a pretty nervous lot. Some that it would go off and some that it wouldnt. The thing I remember my father saying was that he put his hands over his goggles against the initial flare of light and that when it came he could see the bones in his fingers with his eyes closed. There was no sound. Just this searing white light. And then the reddish purple cloud rising in billows and flowering into the iconic white mushroom. Symbol of the age. The whole thing standing slowly to ten thousand feet. The wind from the shockwave was supersonic and it hurt your ears for just a moment. And lastly of course the sound of it. The ungodly detonation followed by the slow rumble, the afterclap that rolled away over the burning countryside into a world that had never existed before this side of the sun. The desert creatures evaporating without a cry and the scientists watching with this thing standing twinned in the black lenses of their goggles. And my father watching it through his fingers like See-No-Evil. But if they knew nothing else they all knew it was too late for that.

What did they say? The scientists.

They all stood up and said Holy Shit.

No they didnt.

I dont think they said anything. They were simply stunned. A friend of my father's, a physicist named Bainbridge who was head of the program, said we're all sons of bitches now. And supposedly Oppenheimer quoted from the Bhagavad Gita but I think the

Sanskrit word for Time came out Death or maybe the other way around. Or maybe they're the same.

I'd have thought that the signature image of our age might better be the NASA photograph of the earth taken from space. That beautiful blue sphere turning in the void.

Interesting juxtaposition, isnt it?

You dont find that photograph moving?

I find it frightening. The void has no stake in the world's continuing existence. It's home as well to countless millions of meteorites. Some of them enormous. Trundling across the blackness at forty miles a second. I think if there were anything to care it would have cared by now. A friend of mine once said: When all trace of our existence is gone, for whom then will this be a tragedy? Do you play those things back or do you just save them?

The tapes.

The tapes. Yes.

Sometimes I play something back. Is that okay?

Sure.

Your father. He never expressed remorse? Or anything like it?

No. A lot of the scientists did. They had second thoughts. My father said that they should have thought of that sooner. They should have had first thoughts.

Would it have made any difference?

No. That was his point. Nothing would have made any difference. There was a movement early on to let the scientists have a say in whether the bomb would be deployed but my father thought they were just naive. He said that the bomb belonged to the people who had paid for it and that certainly wasnt the scientists. They paid for us, he said. We were cheap too. He told them to stop their whining.

Both of your parents died of cancer.

Yes. I dont think the work at Y-12 was particularly hazardous—although my grandmother was convinced that it killed my mother. My father's work in the South Pacific on the other hand was probably close to suicidal. Of course radiation wasnt understood all that well at the time. I suppose some people will find a moral there.

I take it you would not. You said that your father died in a cabin above Lake Tahoe.

No, I said he lived there. It was very beautiful. There was a point of rocks where you could walk out and see the lake maybe twenty miles away below you. But that's not where he died. He died in Juarez Mexico.

He died in Mexico.

Yes.

What was he doing in Mexico?

He went there for cancer treatment.

To Juarez Mexico?

Yes. There was an extract made from apricot pits called Laetrile that was being used in clinics in third world countries. I think they called it vitamin B_{17}. A lot of desperate people showed up at these places. Including not a few celebrities.

Your father went to Mexico to be treated for cancer by quack doctors.

Yes.

That doesnt seem odd to you?

Of course it does. But he'd exhausted all other avenues. I dont think he was particularly hopeful about it. I think he thought about it in probabilistic terms and he couldnt find a way to calculate it down to zero. So he went. If there was a fault in his reasoning it was that he was too well informed to actually put much faith in the curative powers of apricots. And the only chance for it to work would have been if he could.

As in the placebo effect.

As in.

He died in Mexico.

Yes.

Where is he buried?

Somewhere in Mexico. He'd asked my brother to go with him but he wouldnt. He went by himself and he died by himself and he's buried somewhere in Mexico but we dont know where.

Are you all right?

I'm all right. Give me a minute.

———

Okay?

I'm okay.

Why wouldnt your brother go with him?

Because he thought it made my father look foolish.

Did you think that he should have gone?

Yes. So did he. After it was too late.

Was your father an atheist?

Odd question. Are you?

Sometimes. Was he?

I dont know. Probably. I think he considered a person's beliefs a part of his character. He wouldnt have thought that to believe in God—or not—would be a conscious decision. You were probably either a believer or you werent. I'm sure he thought that he was too young to die, but I'm not sure how the Godless deal with death.

Would that include you?

You're just going to get idiosyncratic responses. What's the point?

I'll take what I can get.

If you dont know what life is—and you dont—then I'm not sure how you would characterize the absence of it. I suppose we think that we know where we are but that is obviously absurd. To die is difficult, but to die without knowing where it is that you have been. Or why. Well. Anyway, I'm guessing that what you're trying to come to grips with is what sort of mind would dedicate itself to blowing up the world.

What I'm trying to come to grips with is you. Your brother was remorseful about not going to Mexico with your father.

Remorseful doesnt really say it. My father finally came to him in a dream and after that my brother went to Mexico to see if he could find him.

After your father was dead.

Yes. He went to see if he could find where he was buried.

We can talk about something else.

Maybe it's just not a good day. I'm all right. Go ahead.

Did he find your father's grave?

No.

How long was he in Mexico?

I dont know. I couldnt get hold of him. When I finally found him he was . . . He was in terrible pain. He'd come back to El Paso. I got him to go with me to a restaurant but he couldnt stop crying and he was crying in the restaurant. I put my hand on his arm but he pulled it away.

Why did he do that?

It's complicated.

All right.

He'd found the clinic but they wouldnt talk to him. He wound up giving away all his money to Mexican officials but nothing came of it. He was there for weeks. Sleeping in a three dollar hotel. I dont know when he'd eaten last. He looked like a ghost.

This was in El Paso.

Yes. He was at the Gardner Hotel when he finally called me. He'd had another dream. Except that he didnt call it a dream. What he said was that our father had come to him in the night and that he'd stood at his bedfoot in his deathclothes and my brother kept asking him where he was but he didnt know. He didnt know where he was. My brother told me this in tears over the phone and then he hung up and I thought that he would take his life.

He never found where your father was buried.

No.

Was all of this as distressing to you as it was to your brother?

It was more than distressing. It is yet. But I hadnt refused to help my father. I hadnt been asked. Mostly I was worried about Bobby. He was in terrible shape.

You really thought he might kill himself.

Yes. I didnt know what I would find when I got there.

And if he had killed himself?

I dont know. I think I probably would have killed myself as quickly as possible and then tried to find him.

You're joking.

I dont think so.

Do you believe in an afterlife?

I dont believe in this one.

Do you?

I've no idea. It strikes me as extremely unlikely. But again the probability is not zero.

We've never really talked about why you came back to Stella Maris.

I'd nowhere else to go.

I find it hard to believe that you'd have come here if you hadnt been looking for help of some sort.

If you like.

There are limits to this conversation, arent there? You dont want to jeopardize your walk in the woods? You're smiling.

Sorry.

No, it's all right. Whatever my concerns about you, keeping you alive has to be at the head of the list.

What else?

Did Bobby ever go back to Mexico?

No.

Did your father ever come to him again? Isnt that how he put it?

No, he didnt.

I've asked you this before but were you close to your father?

No. But I loved him. Then and now.

We've just a few more minutes. Tell me something odd about yourself.

Something odd.

Yes.

You're asking me what's odd about me?

Yes. Something I might not know. It could even be something trivial.

All right.

Well?

I'm thinking.

Okay.

I can tell time backwards.

What do you mean?

I mean that if I see a clock in a mirror I know what time it is.

So do I.

No you dont. You have to stop and figure it out.

And you dont.

And I dont.

You trained yourself to do this.

I just thought about it.

How did you think about it?

At first I just folded it over. Visually. Like a page.

In your mind. Sorry.

And then after a while I didnt have to fold it over. I could just see it.

What else.

What else what?

I dont know. What else about clocks.

In the mirror the three and the nine reverse in their locations but not the six and the twelve. It's a child's question but some grown-ups have a problem with it. If you throw a handful of sticks in the air and photograph them there will be a lot more sticks oriented in the horizontal plane than in the vertical. Why is that? After all, they have the same degrees of freedom.

I dont know.

It's because a stick rotating in the vertical passes through the horizontal plane midway. And briefly becomes a member. Twice. But a horizontal stick in its rotation has nothing to contribute to the vertical plane. Doesnt seem fair, does it? Images in a closing glass door rotate but they cant bend. Optics. Handedness. Chirality. Color. Questions everywhere.

Why did you become a mathematician rather than a physicist?

Because it was harder. Maybe. Mostly because whatever else physical reality may be it is finite.

This may be the most animated I've seen you.

Well. Take a good look.

The violin.

Yes.

You couldnt find time to practice you said.

Probably I didnt really think that I was good enough. To be honest. At one point I was interested in the mathematics of the violin. I corresponded with a woman in New Jersey named Carleen Hutchins who was trying to map the harmonics of the instrument. She'd taken any number of rare Cremonas apart with a soldering iron. She worked with some physicists setting up some rather elaborate equipment to establish the Chladni patterns of the plates. But the vibrations and frequencies were so complex that they resisted any complete analysis. I thought that I could do mathematical models of these frequency patterns.

Did you?

Yes.

What did you find out?

Carleen kept good records. The oldest known violin is an Amati believed to be from 1564 that's in the Ashmolean at Oxford. The oldest instrument we studied was from 1580 and the latest was probably a German violin from the 1960s. Aside from the angle of the neck they were the same. Nothing had changed. Nothing.

That seems rather remarkable.

Yes. What's even more remarkable is that there is no prototype to the violin. It simply appears out of nowhere in all its perfection.

And what do you make of that? You've told me this for a reason.

It's just another mystery to add to the roster. Leonardo cant be explained. Or Newton, or Shakespeare. Or endless others. Well. Probably not endless. But at least we know their names. But unless you're willing to concede that God invented the violin there is a figure who will never be known. A small man who went with his son into the stunted forests of the little iceage of fifteenth century Italy and sawed and split the maple trees and put the flitches to dry for seven years and then stood in the slant light of his shop one morning and said a brief prayer of thanks to his creator and then— knowing this perfect thing—took up his tools and turned to its construction. Saying now we begin.

I'm sorry. This gentleman is very close to your heart.

Sorry. Yes. Very close. Time's up.

V

I thought perhaps you werent coming.

It took my keepers longer than we thought to get me out of my restraints.

Have you ever been in restraints?

No. Discounting electroshock therapy.

You've never been late before.

No. Just absent.

You seem to rather make a point of it.

Punctuality.

Yes.

I do.

Are you all right with everything?

Yeah. Sure.

You're not upset.

No. I sleep with the lights on anyway. For the most part.

What dictates that? About the lights.

I suppose it's just what's on the road.

In the sense of something coming?

In the sense.

Is this a recurring fantasy?

Why is it a fantasy?

Something approaching in the dark.

Yes.

And you think that with the lights on you'll be safer.

Or it will be easier for them to find me.

You're not serious.

Probably not.

But you do think that there could be things in the dark that intend you harm.

Yes. Dont you?

I'm afraid I dont.

Well. People have been afraid of the dark for a long time. The dark in every sense of it. They've always attributed a will to the forces of malevolence. Then suddenly in our day war and famine and pestilence are just random events. Is that a comfort to you?

I wouldnt particularly want to live in a world governed by superstition. I think things have improved. I think in fact that they've improved a good deal.

Because of science.

I'm not sure that it's all science.

No? Name one thing about the world that makes it a better place than the world of 1900 that isnt due to science.

I'll have to think about it.

It's all right. I'm just being confrontational.

You were put on suicide watch the last time because of your seeming obsession with death.

It says.

Dr Horowitz says. Was there some particular incident that alarmed him?

I think I just made him nervous. I'm not sure what he thought. He wasnt all that forthcoming. Sometimes he would just sit and watch me.

Like he was trying to figure you out?

I dont know. Maybe more like trying to intimidate me. He never understood that there was nothing to intimidate. I would just say whatever it was that I was thinking. It really didnt make that much difference whether he was even there. Or not. The therapist has to believe that the patient is the doctor. That she contains the truth regarding herself. What do you think?

I suppose I would agree with that.

I think I was just a frustrating experience for Dr Horowitz. Is he a friend of yours?

I know him. Not well. You've never really spent much time with people.

Such as who?

I dont know. Anybody. People that you care about. Did you spend time with your brother?

Yes. As much as I could. I think I always knew what was coming.

Well. Sometimes people think that. After what was coming has arrived. How do you think that you knew?

I just did. I didnt make it up after the fact.

But you dont want to talk about your brother.

No.

Do you think that you're honest with people?

Meaning you.

Okay. Me.

You have your doubts I take it.

Well. I'm not tracking down facts so much as trying to see what you think.

Are you just another Horowitz to me.

I dont think that. The doubts I have would be mostly that if you were in trouble you might not be forthcoming about it.

That's what Bobby used to say.

Was he right?

Yes.

You didnt want him to worry.

I didnt want him to worry.

You resent people wanting to help you.

I resent people wanting to fix me.

Would that describe your brother?

Sometimes. I think. It pains me to say.

Did you think that he should have taken you to Europe with him?

I got there anyway.

I know. But that wasnt the question.

I know. But that's the answer.

You dont want to talk about it.

Him.

I just wondered if he shared your pessimism.

Not really. Or maybe he took it as part of his job to try and cheer me up. If anything I was always more inclined to metaphysical musings than he was. Is all of reality devoid of sentience? I dont know. But he would think the question inane.

Do you mean that the world itself might be possessed of something like a will?

Something like. And would that really be good news? That every dumb creature that ever found itself called into being in order to trek its way across a landscape of pain and want to its ultimate eternal extinction is that will's handiwork?

But the answer, or the solution, could hardly be more of the same.

Hardly.

How many books have you read?

Crikey.

Crikey?

I dont know. Not that many.

Roughly.

Probably two a day. On average. For ten years or so. We'll say. What is that? Seven thousand three hundred. Is that a lot? It's probably more. Probably more like ten thousand. I think I'm going to go for ten thousand. Sometimes I would read all day. Eighteen, twenty hours.

Do you remember everything you read?

Yes. Why else would you read it?

Does the Kid know what you know?

No. That would be a bit easy, wouldnt it?

What sorts of things would he talk about.

It was mostly nonsense. Interspersed with comments that were pretty interesting. Sometimes. But mostly talk that you might characterize as schizoid. Klang associations. Rhyming. None of which echoed my own interior life. Before you ask. But having to put up with his dog and pony show was wearing. To say the least. And I'm sure it changed me. You cant have your ambient reality put askew without becoming somewhat askew yourself. By the time that sank in it was too late to do anything about it. But then it was always too late anyway. Even if there was something to be done. Which there wasnt.

So what might he say? For instance?

He might say that milk is the beverage of choice among all right-thinking nightfolk. Or he would say that if anything were true wouldnt everybody know it by now? Or that you shouldnt worry about what people think of you because they dont do it that often. Or that we are hardly creatures of the light in case you hadnt noticed. Or that the darkest hour is just before the storm. Or when you close your eyes do I go away? Do you?

Did he?

Yes. Me too.

That's the general tenor of it?

If you've grasped the general tenor of it you're way ahead of me. He'd talk about science but he would usually get it wrong. He liked to quote but he would get that wrong too. He'd sometimes affect accents but they were pretty bad. Or he'd quote passages from texts that I'm pretty sure didnt exist. There was a book on female sexuality called *The Damp and the Angry* that he cited several times. Try looking that up. He would talk about upcoming acts. Which never materialized. Quaint phrasing.

Acts.

Yes.

What kind of acts?

Things he would put together. Vaudeville acts. Chautauquas. That never showed up of course. Things like The Gypsy from Poughkeepsie. Or The Barnfowl Follies featuring the Rooster from Worcester. Coming attractions that never arrived. If I brought it up he'd pace up and back and wave his flippers around. He said that you could hardly expect these high-end acts to appear at the snap of a finger. He'd try and snap his fingers but of course he didnt have any and he'd just sort of flap his flippers.

What else.

Nothing much. He'd wind up spouting some sort of gibberish. It would be nice to think that there was actual data encoded in these spiels but I've been listening to them for years and Turing couldnt untangle them. We did actually have a minstrel show early on. When I was twelve. They announced it as the menstrual show. In honor of. All of it wretched beyond telling. Most of the time I'd just curl up in bed and work on math problems. Sometimes I'd look up and everybody would be gone except him. Still pacing. He'd go over the books on my shelf and suggest further reading. All of it nonsense of course. Some of it funny. Probably not to him. I certainly never saw him laugh. Just this bogus yukking he would do. I told him once that he was wasting his time. That I wanted to be a warrior. Not a being of the spirit but of the flesh. I was a born classicist and my heroes were never saints but killers. He would look quite serious and then hold forth with a diatribe concerning the longheld strongholds of rugmold.

Did you come to see him as something of a guardian? That's an odd question. I suppose.

I think in the end I came to see him as what I was left with. That's not very reassuring is it? Well. No. It's not.

Do you ever have dreams about him?

As in whether his ersatz reality might speak against his admission to my dreamscape?

Something like that. Ersatz reality?

You can call it something else.

Do you have troubling dreams?

Is there some other kind?

Do you?

Yes. I have troubling dreams.

Any thoughts about that?

Sure. This little slut has thoughts about everything. And opinions, dont forget.

Is that me?

No. Just me.

I've touched a raw nerve.

Is there some other kind? Sorry. It's just that if we're going to talk about my dream-life we're going to have to start over. Maybe get up and leave the room and come back in different clothes.

What are you going to wear?

Something diaphanous. Cloud blue I think. You?

Do you remember them? Your dreams?

Pretty much. The ones that wake you, of course.

Why do some dreams wake you?

They think you've had enough?

Supposedly you're being told something. But you're not told what to do about it, are you?

The dream wakes us to tell us to remember. Maybe there's nothing to be done. Maybe the question is whether the terror is a warning about the world or about ourselves. The night world from which you are brought upright in your bed gasping and sweating. Are you waking from something you have seen or from something that you are?

Is that the question?

Or maybe the real question is simply why the mind seems bent upon convincing us of the reality of that which has none.

You said at some point that the unconscious was reluctant to communicate with us linguistically. For historical reasons? Do I have that right?

Yes.

Would you like to elaborate on that?

I dont think so. Psychiatrists have trouble dealing with the unconscious in a straightforward way. But the unconscious is a purely biological system, not a magical one. It's a biological system because that's all there is for it to be. People arent happy talking about the unconscious unless there's a certain amount of hokum involved. But there isnt. The unconscious is simply a machine for operating an animal. What else could it be? Most of what we do is unconscious. Turning chores over to the conscious mind is a risky business. Whales and dolphins have to time their breathing to their surfacing. So of course when they were first anesthetized for surgery they simply died. Which should have been predictable. The unconscious evolves along with the species to meet its needs and if there's anything spooky about it it's that it sometimes seems to anticipate those needs. It cant afford surprises. It's one of the things that troubled Darwin. But the souldoctors dont get any of this. They're Cartesian to the bone.

So how do they sleep?

Dolphins.

Yes.

Rather well, I would imagine. Guiltless creatures that they are.

No. I meant . . .

They sleep one hemisphere of their brain at a time.

Is that true?

Christ in a crinoline. As the Kid would say.

Sorry. Dont they sink to the bottom?

You're forgetting that they're half awake. Or that half of them is awake. The interesting thing to contemplate is whether the waking brain is privy to the sleeping brain's dreams. Or does the corpus callosum shut down at night? Or why is a dying dolphin's last breath not an act of suicide. Actually the one after the last. The one he refuses to take.

Maybe we should sally back to the dayworld.

Sally it is.

We seem to have misplaced the metaphysical.

Probably just as well.

Do you think that the sense of self is an illusion?

Well. I think you know that the consensus among the neural folk is yes. I think it's a dumb question. Coherent entities composed of a great number of disparate parts arent—as a general rule—thereby assumed to have their identities compromised. I know that seems to be ignoring our sense of ourselves as a single being. The "I." I just think it's a silly way of viewing things. If we were constructed with a continual awareness of how we worked we wouldnt work. You might even ask that if the self is indeed an illusion for whom then is it illusory? I thought we were going to ditch the mind for a while?

Fair enough. You were raised by your grandmother from the age of what? Twelve?

Yes.

Are you estranged from her?

No. Of course not.

But you've had your differences.

She didnt know what to do with me. It wasnt her fault. I didnt either. I thought when I left for college she'd breathe a sigh of relief. I was too preoccupied with my own problems to see hers. She drove me to the bus station in Knoxville. I had one suitcase and it was mostly books. I turned on the platform to hug her and she was crying and I realized that she was terrified.

Terrified.

Yes.

For you.

For me. Yes.

You were how old?

I was fourteen.

You left the university after two years.

Yes. I'd graduated.

In two years.

Plus the summers. It wasnt hard. I was admitted to the doctoral program but then I packed up and moved to Tucson Arizona. I worked in a bar at night and did math all day.

When did you sleep?

I slept about five hours a day. Four.

You werent old enough to tend bar. You werent old enough to even be in a bar.

I had the bogus driver's license.

Where was the Kid?

He showed up after a while. My little dybbuk and his friends. My brother had given me a car and I used to drive up into the mountains and sit with my feet in the creek and work problems in algebraic topology. I'd read Noether's papers and they were pretty straightforward. Poincaré of course. What the Betti groups actually meant. The homology groups. But it was how she got there. Aside from the fact that she knew more abstract algebra than anybody else. I knew that in order to do what she'd done you would first have to believe it. But this seemed different. Intuition is a tough nut to crack. The cool thing about topology is that the problems you are working on are not about something else. Your hope is that in solving them they will explain to you why you were asking them. You're tracking down the affine. Can you really stretch a surface any way you like? What if you stretched it to infinity? The width would narrow infinitely. Can the limits of the infinitesimal be approached forever? The mathematics may say yes but you dont believe it. Infinite extension is just more of the same but infinite contraction seems to present a different set of problems. In the classical understanding. You're in Zeno land. Begin again and concentrate.

I dont know what any of that means.

It's all right. Add to your troubles the idea that topology has questionable mathematical foundations—or none at all, as some of its founders believed—and then what? You can say that it contains its own logic, but isnt that the problem? If you claim that mathematics is not a science then you can claim that it need have no referent save itself. When Wittgenstein convinced Russell that all of mathematics was a tautology Russell gave up mathematics.

Is that true?

I dont know. Russell said it was.

Would that be your view?

I dont think the question can be answered. For the present I guess I'd have to say no. But by then I'd already left the building. And the deeper question, which we touched on, is that if mathematical work is performed mostly in the unconscious we still have no notion as to how it goes about it. You can try and picture the inner mind adding and subtracting and muttering and erasing and beginning again but you wont get very far. And why is it so often right? Who does it check its work with? I've had solutions to problems simply handed to me. Out of the blue. The locus ceruleus perhaps. And it has to remember everything. No notes. It's hard to escape the unsettling conclusion that it's not using numbers.

I dont understand how that would be possible.

That might not be true. That it is that often right. What's probably true is that only the right answers get reported. At a conference a while back I ran into the historian of the Manhattan Project. A man named David Hawkins. We got to talking about math and he told me that what first got him interested in the subject was the second chapter of Spengler's *Decline of the West.* Which is entitled "The Meaning of Numbers." I asked him what Spengler's view was and he said that he wasnt sure. That Spengler seemed eager to make a distinction between mathematics as numeracy and mathematics as chronology. Which I thought was already pretty well established in the cardinal and the ordinal but I assumed that Spengler was after something else. But I got the book and read the opening chapter and a bit more here and there. As with the general run of philosophers—if he is one—the most interesting thing was not his ideas but just the way his mind worked. I read a bit more before I gave it up but I thought it one of the more interesting pieces of nonsense I'd come across. I dont think you can call him a crank. He knows too much. And it really is well written. I think I would put him with Schopenhauer as an exemplar of German prose. He makes some odd statements. The mathematics of night? I suppose Grothendieck is capable of saying something like that. But Grothendieck is a great mathematician. You have to take him seriously. Beginning this lengthy study of what he takes to be the meaning of history with an inquiry into the meaning of mathematics is a strategy that modern philosophers might well take into consideration. An enormous amount of Wittgenstein's work is in mathematics. Very little of it published.

Does Spengler know any math?

I dont know. He never mentions anyone. It's all just notional. I dont know how you can write about the meaning of numbers with no mention of Frege. Even in 1917 or '19. But even Frege doesnt get completely down to nuts and bolts. Adding and subtracting are not really mathematics. A sack of pebbles will do. But multiplication and division are a different matter. If you were to multiply two tomatoes by two tomatoes you wouldnt get four tomatoes. You would get four tomatoes squared. So what is the two? Well. It's an independent abstract mathematical operator. Oh? And what is that?

We dont know. We made it up. Do you remember any of this from Math 101?

I'm not sure I see the point.

I know. The actual issue is that someone a hundred thousand years ago sat up in his robes and said Holy Shit. Sort of. He didnt have a language yet. But what he had just understood is that one thing can be another thing. Not look like it or act upon it. Be it. Stand for it. Pebbles can be goats. Sounds can be things. The name for water is water. What seems inconsequential to us by reason of usage is in fact the founding notion of civilization. Language, art, mathematics, everything. Ultimately the world itself and all in it.

And the greatest of these I take it is mathematics.

Well. I'm a mathematician.

So is God a mathematician?

God cant add two and two. Zero and one are all he's got to work with. The rest is us. Kronecker notwithstanding. Maybe we should shelve this for a while.

Okay. When you left school and went to Arizona did you leave the doctoral program?

No. I still hear from them occasionally.

They want to know how things are going.

They want to know how things are going.

I take it that you have a faculty advisor.

I do. I dont ever hear from her.

Did you have a falling-out?

No. But I dont really trust her.

Why is that?

I would find her agreeing with things that I knew she didnt understand. And I made her nervous.

A common theme in your life?

I suppose.

In your mathematical life?

Not so much. Mathematicians tend to be pretty straightforward. I think a lot of them dont really even understand the idea of dissimulation. They're an odd lot, more oddly taken. Chaitin said that he was asked once if he had any connection to real life. They wanted to know if he read the newspapers.

How did your work go? In Tucson.

It took pretty much the same path as any doomed enterprise. It would move along on a gradual downward slope and then drop precipitously.

I take it this was somewhat discouraging.

Not really. I knew that what I was after was there. Doing math is a bit like selling door to door. You have to learn to handle rejection. I went through Hilbert's problems. Not to solve them but to try to find out what if anything they had in common. Mathematics was spreading out and as it was spreading out it was thinning out. Sometime in the early twentieth century it finally became impossible for anyone to understand all of it. Cantor supposedly was the last universal mathematician. Then Poincaré. Then no one. Anyway, there were times when I considered that my career might be over. And at the same time I never questioned my ability. I was the best mathematician I knew.

So what happened?

Mathematicians tend to get huffy when you suggest to them that mathematical truths represent a sort of second class reality. When T D Lee was working on non-Abelian gauge theory he came across a mathematics called fiber-bundle theory. And the two theories were the same. So he went to his mathematics friends and asked them to explain this but they didnt see what needed explaining. But Lee said that while the gauge theory was a physical theory and therefore real the fiber-bundle theory was not a physical theory and therefore not real. And they got upset and they said no no no it is real. Topology is able to describe with some precision forms that belie physical exemplification. Yet they cant be ideations because then you have to ask ideations of what? Anyway, by the end of the summer I had more or less dug myself into a hole.

All right. So what happened?

Three wise men came from the East.

I'm sorry?

I got a fellowship to IHES and there I met three men that I could talk to.

This is the Institute in France.

Yes.

Who were the men?

Grothendieck, Deligne, and Oscar Zariski.

Why them?

Because it was them, because it was me.

That sounds like a quote.

It is. Montaigne.

Your faculty advisor. Did she consider you . . . Not sure about the word. Somewhat grandiose?

I suppose. Of course she wasnt offered a fellowship at IHES.

This was quite prestigious I take it.

Yes.

You had never met Grothendieck.

No. I wrote him a letter and he said to send him a paper and I did.

What was the paper about?

It was an explication of topos theory that I thought he probably hadnt considered. And he hadnt. What I didnt know was that he was already leaving mathematics. I didnt have much time.

Are you all right?

I'm all right.

Do you want to come back to this?

I'm all right.

We can talk about something else. What is it that we've more or less passed over?

The fact that I'm female.

As regards mathematics? Or the souldoctors.

Either one.

The doctors then.

Women enjoy a different history of madness. From witchcraft to hysteria we're just bad news. We know that women were condemned as witches because they were mentally unstable but no one has considered the numbers—even few as they might be—of women who were stoned to death for being bright. That I havent wound up chained to a cellar wall or burned at the stake is not a testament to our ascending civility but to our ascending skepticism. If we still believed in witches we'd still be burning them. Hooknosed crones strapped into the electric chair. No one has ever seemed to comment that the stereotypical witch is meant to appear Jewish. I guess the skepticism is okay. If you can stomach what goes with it. I'm happy to be treated well but I know that it's an uncertain business. When this world which reason has created is carried off at last it will take reason with it. And it will be a long time coming back. What happened to our turns?

I guess I thought it was just a device. To get us started. Go ahead.

Antique phrase.

Go ahead?

Yes. Have you ever lost a patient to suicide?

Yes. Once.

A young woman.

Yes.

Did you attend the funeral?

Odd question. Yes. I did.

How did that go?

About like you'd expect. Or worse. No one would speak to me.

Did you think they would?

I hoped they would. I was just trying to do what I thought was right. I could see it their way. An unpleasant figure lurking in the corner. An unwelcome guest. I'd never seen people so ruined by grief. You become accustomed to people's gratitude. You take it for granted. Thank you Doctor. You dont think about it. But blame is deep and abiding. I stood around in my black suit for a while and then I left. Is it still your turn?

Did you ever consider some other life? Some other place?

I guess some other life would have to be some other place. I dont know. Maybe not. Another life? Some other career?

Or no life.

That would be you, not me.

You're pretty happy.

I'm pretty happy.

When I was a child I used to daydream about living in some far-away place. I was always plotting how to get there.

An imaginary place or a real one?

I think you start with the imaginary. Later you get serious and you dig out the atlas.

Where did you wind up?

Here.

You didnt find Stella Maris in the atlas.

I know. It was Romania.

Romania.

Yes.

Why?

It's where my family was from. My mother's family. Bobby researched it. The woman who landed at Ellis Island in 1848 was fifteen. She'd left Europe with her mother but her mother never arrived. She wasnt on the debarkation list. There was no explanation on the manifest but she had to have died at sea. Did this girl have anyone to meet her? I dont know.

How did she wind up in Tennessee? Or did she?

I dont know that either. She seems to have been married by the time she was sixteen. Bobby tried to find out about her family in Europe. Our family. There wasnt much. The Europe she fled was pledged to endless war. There were Jewish families that walked across Asia to ports on the Russian coast. Carrying their suitcases. When Bobby told Uncle Royal that we were Jews Uncle Royal ordered him out of the house.

Did he go?

No. Of course not.

This is the nutty uncle.

Yes.

He's an Anti-Semite.

Anti-Semitism is the least of his problems.

Is that a family name? Royal?

No. We just have weird names in the south. Could have been Raoul originally. I know. Royal is a legitimate name. And of course you get a lot of Spanish names. In Tennessee anyway. Carlos. Wanita. With a W.

Where did they come from?

They were brought back from the Mexican War. Along with hot tamales. He climbed into bed with me one night.

Your uncle?

Yes.

What did you do?

I climbed out and went to the door and called down to my grandmother.

What did he do?

He jumped up and ran out the door. In his shorts. Skinny.

How old were you?

Thirteen.

Did you tell your grandmother?

No. She had enough problems. When I came down the next

morning I told him that I still hadnt decided whether or not to tell Bobby. That sobered him up.

Did you tell Bobby?

God no. Bobby would have killed him.

Your brother was very protective of you.

Yes. Very.

He never climbed into bed with you.

My brother? No. It was the other way around.

That's not true.

I never climbed into bed with my brother.

Why did he take up racing cars?

Because he was good at it. And he suddenly had the money to do it with. My grandmother hated it. But still she kept all the clippings. Physicists tend to have hobbies that are hazardous to their health. A lot of them are mountain climbers. Sometimes with predictable results. He went to England and bought a Formula Two Lotus from the factory.

I take it that's the car that he crashed in Italy.

Why dont we move on.

All right. Sorry. Romania.

Yes.

Did you really want to go and live there?

Yes. I did.

What about your brother?

Well. That was the plan.

You thought that your brother would go and live in Romania with you?

I hoped that he would. Yes.

What did he say?

He said that it was not exactly what he had in mind.

What else.

It's complicated.

What was your relationship with your brother?

What do you think?

I dont know.

I dont either. Are you asking me if we did it?

Did you?

No.

What else?

On this subject?

Yes.

Love is quite possibly a mental disorder itself.

Is that a serious comment?

Yes.

Do you believe that?

Probably. Maybe not. Sometimes. The literature is not encouraging. Nor experience.

Are you telling me that you were in love with your brother?

Well, as a good shrink you probably believe that incest is the way to a girl's heart.

But it wasnt incest.

No. Just longing.

You dont want to talk about this.

Affairs of the heart are entitled to some confidentiality.

All right.

I knew that I wasnt supposed to be in Wartburg Tennessee and I thought it possible that Bobby had found where it was that I was supposed to be. Where we were supposed to be.

You were serious.

Yes. I'd even found a grammar and started in on the language.

Did you know what part of the country your family was from?

No. I wanted to live in the mountains. Not too far from a town of reasonable size. Maybe even Bucharest. I needed a library. I wanted to live near a river and have a canoe.

A canoe.

It's pathetic, isnt it?

I dont know what it is. For how long did you entertain this fantasy?

I entertain it yet.

Do you want to stop?

Sorry. No. I'm all right.

You lived in Europe but you never visited Romania.

I didnt want to visit. I wanted to go there.

Maybe we should stop.

A deal's a deal. A little hysteria shouldnt be cause for a breach of contract.

We could talk about something else.

Shoes and ships and sealing wax.

Do you ever plan these discussions beforehand?

I'm sure I wasnt the first kid to wonder why anyone would want to wax their ceiling. No. I just wing it. Same as you.

I give it some thought. Jot down a few notes.

What are your plans for the tapes?

To do a paper, if everything goes well. I think that was the agreement.

Just as long as I dont have to read it.

Were you this pessimistic about the world from an early age?

Like it was all sunshine and light prior to pubescence?

I dont know.

I dont think people are wrong to be concerned about the world's intentions toward them. There's a lot of bad news out there and some of it is coming to your house.

Drowning yourself in Lake Tahoe. Was that a serious consideration?

Pretty serious. I guess that's in there.

It's mentioned. But you decided against it.

Yes.

What changed your mind?

Girls dont like to be cold.

Seriously.

I sat down and thought about it.

No surprise there.

I went through the physiology of it. It wasnt very reassuring.

Do you want to talk about that?

Sure. What the hell.

We have some time.

Well. The first thing you come to understand is that the panic attendant to suffocation is atavistic. It's as old as the brain and there's nothing you can do about it. You might think that you can screw your courage up to deal with it but you cant. It overrides all reason. It's a thing we share with rats. You could say that fear of falling is also primitive, but climbers who have fallen to what they believed to be their deaths universally report calm and acceptance. Why is that?

I dont know.

I think it's because there's no decision to be made.

Decision.

Yes. If you're drowning then at some point you're going to have to make the decision to breathe in the water and die. You may think that the decision will be made for you, but even if you cant hold your breath for another second you can hold it another millisecond. And of course it's not a choice but a decision. You have to make the decision to kill yourself. There's nothing like that in falling to your death. The movies dont get that right either. There's no kicking and screaming. You're absolved of all responsibility. You're quits. Are you sure about these morbid conversations?

It's up to you.

Okay. My thought was to rent a boat. I was sitting in the pine woods above the lake and I thought about the incredible clarity of the water and I could see that was a plus. You really dont want to drown yourself in muddy water. It's something people ought to think about. I saw myself sitting in the boat with the oars shipped.

At some point I would take a last look around. I would have a heavy leather belt and a goodsized padlock from the hardware store and I would have fastened myself to the chain of the anchor through the belt where it doubles after passing through the buckle. Click the padlock shut and drop the key over the side. Maybe row off a few strokes. You dont want to be down there on the bottom scrambling around looking for a key. You take one last look and lift the anchor into your lap and swing your feet over the side and push off into eternity. The work of an instant. The work of a lifetime.

But you didnt.

I didnt. First of all the water off the east shore is about sixteen hundred feet deep and agonizingly cold. A number of things are going to happen that you hadnt taken into consideration. Of course if you had you wouldnt be there in the first place. Or the last. As you descend, your lungs will start to shrivel. At a thousand feet they'll be about the size of tennisballs. You try to clear your ears and that hurts. Your eardrums in all likelihood are going to burst and that is really going to hurt. There is a technique for bringing up air and forcing it through the eustachian tubes into your ears but you arent going to have the air to do it with. So you drift down in your thin chain of bubbles. The mountains draw away. The receding sun and the painted bottom of the boat. The world. Your heart slows to a tick. Dive deep enough and it will stop altogether. The blood is leaving your extremities to pool in your lungs. But the biggest problem is just coming. You're going to run out of air before you reach the bottom of the lake. Even with a sixty pound anchor—about all I could manage—you're not going to make very good time. At twelve miles an hour—which is pretty fast—you're doing a thousand feet a minute. Under the circumstances that you've chosen for yourself a breath may not last a minute. Even if you've done the fast respirations before you committed. The shock and the stress and the cold and the diminishing air supply are going to take their toll. Anyway, it's going to be a good two minute trip to the bottom and probably more like four or five. Not sitting comfortably on the bottom of the lake.

Comfortably.

Sure. At least you'd finally be able to put down that bloody anchor.

Did you enjoy working all this out?

Why not? Problems are always fun.

I dont always know when you're serious.

I know. Anyway, at this juncture you'll have dropped the anchor and it is going to be towing you by your belt down through water that is freezing your brain. It's unlikely you'll be able to keep your wits about you but it really doesnt matter. When you finally give up your rat's struggle and breath in the water—scaldingly cold—you are going to experience pain beyond the merely agonizing. Maybe it will distract you from the mental anguish at what you have done to yourself, I dont know. See if you can remember the pain in your lungs from being out of breath from running on a cold winter day. You're breathing in quicker than your lungs can warm the air. It hurts. Now multiply that by God knows what. The heat content of water as compared to that of air. And it's not going to go away. Because your lungs can never warm the water they've inhaled. I think we're talking about an agony that is simply off the scale. No one's ever said. And it's forever. Your forever.

You're sitting in the woods above the lake on a lovely spring day and these are your thoughts.

These are them.

What else.

There are still unknowns here, of course. The bottom of the lake will be pretty much gravel so there wont be any billowing silt when the anchor touches down. Total silence. No telling what's down there. The corpses of those who have gone before. A family you didnt know you had. It's deep enough that the light is pretty dim for all the clarity of the water. A cold gray world. Not black yet. No life. The only color is the thin pink stain trailing away in the water from the blood leaking out of your ears. We dont know about the gag reflex but we're fixing to find out.

Fixing.

Fixing. Once your lungs are full will this abate? The gagging? Dont know. No one's ever said. The autonomous reflex will be to cough out the water but you cant because it's too heavy. And of course there's nothing to replace it with anyway except more water. In the meantime oxygen deprivation and nitrogen narcosis have begun to compete for your sanity. You're sitting on the glacial floor of the lake with the weight of the water in your lungs like a cannonball and the pain of the cold in your chest is probably indistinguishable from fire and you are gagging in agony and even though your mind is beginning to go you are yet caught in the iron grip of a terror utterly atavistic and over which you have no control whatsoever and now out of nowhere there's a new thought. The extraordinary cold is probably capable of keeping you alive for an unknown period of time. Hours perhaps, drowned or not. And you may well assume that you will be unconscious but do you know that? What if you're not? As the reasons for not doing to yourself what you have just irrevocably done accumulate in your head you will be left weeping and gibbering and praying to be in hell. Anyway, sitting there among the trees in the soft wind I knew that I would not be going there. Maybe I had been a bad person in my life, but I hadnt been that bad. I stood up and walked back up to my car and drove back to San Francisco.

Had you driven to Lake Tahoe with the express purpose of killing yourself?

Yes.

What else.

Nothing else. I thought about writing up my findings. I thought that people bent on drowning themselves were probably in for some nasty surprises and that what I had to say might change their minds.

Did you analyze other methods of suicide in this way?

Not really. There wasnt that much to analyze. Some things of course are just too brutally painful on the face of it. Setting yourself on fire. For instance.

You wont say whether you feel you are presently at risk.

Of setting myself on fire?

No. I . . .

I'm joking.

Oh.

I thought we'd decided that I was. Or you'd decided.

Where was your brother during this time?

In Italy.

So this was fairly recent.

Yes. You should just ask me what it is that you want to know.

A lot of the time you wont answer. About your brother, particularly.

I know.

What other plans did you entertain for doing away with yourself?

Serious plans?

Any kind. All right, serious.

I'd always had the idea that I didnt want to be found. That if you died and nobody knew about it that would be as close as you could get to never having been here in the first place. I thought about things like motoring out to sea in a rubber raft with a big outboard clamped to the transom and just go till you ran out of gas. Then you would chain yourself to the outboard and take a big handful of pills and open all the valves just very slightly and lie down and go to sleep. You'd probably want a quilt and a pillow. The rubber floor of the raft is going to be cold.

Cold again.

Yes.

Anyway, after a couple of hours or so the thing would just fold up and take you to the bottom of the ocean to be seen no more forever. Stuff like that.

Stuff like that.

Yeah.

Is this an ongoing study?

I shouldnt have told you all this, should I?

Why not.

It's only going to worry you. To no purpose.

Meaning that there's nothing I could do about it.

Well. I dont think there's much that anybody can do about anything.

For all the bleakness of your views you really dont present as clinically depressed.

I know. You said. My cup runneth over.

Is it your belief that your pessimism is based on an understanding of the world not so readily available to other people?

Is this a trick question?

I dont think so.

I think that people in general have a reasonable understanding of the world. I think that if they didnt we wouldnt be here.

Spoken as a Darwinian.

Spoken. Some gifts are unwelcome. I suppose the suspicion is that our common past can only warrant a common future if we are willing to rid ourselves of the outliers. One by one. As they appear. Rid. Confine. Whatever.

Are we approaching the world of the . . . what? The Archatron?

I dont know. Dont look like that. I really dont.

The presence beyond the gate. You must have some sense of it.

Such as what? A vile wind? A darkness?

The Archatron.

I suppose. Originally the Imperator. I was twelve and a fan of language. I saw the gate and the guardians of the gate. I couldnt see beyond.

Did they warn you back?

They did.

How did they warn you?

With a flick of their cold rats' eyes. I saw them through the judas hole that I wasnt supposed to find. But then I hadnt been here before. They were surprised to see me. Anyway, not every view of the world with but a single speculation is thereby a false one. Or a mistaken one. Any number of truths hitherto unknown to us have entered the human domain through the testimony of a single witness.

Do you think maybe people in general hold a fairly dark view of things? Which view they just suppress?

Yes. Dont you?

I dont know.

People prefer fate to chance. Soldiers really do believe that there is a bullet out there with their name on it. I think most people believe not only in a book of life but in a book of their life. Fate can be appeased, gods prayed to. But chance is just what it says.

Do you believe in a book of your life?

Only in the sense that I'm writing it. Which of course could be an illusion. Anyway, it's hardly even a question. Next Thursday at ten AM I will be somewhere. I will be either alive or dead. My presence at that place and at that time is a codlock certainty. A summation of every event in the world. For me. I wont be somewhere else. A lack of foreknowledge doesnt change anything.

Codlock?

Another southernism.

Do you think of yourself as an atheist?

God no. Those were the good old days.

I dont know if that's a serious comment or not.

I know. Me either. What can I tell you? I'm a modern girl.

Well. I've known a few modern girls. I cant say that you fit the profile particularly. Do you want to call it a day?

I look unhappy? Tougher mettle is called for I suppose. I'm all right. For a long time I've suspected that we might be simply incapable of imagining the epochal evils of which we stand rightly accused and I thought it at least a possibility that the structure of reality itself harbors something like the forms of which our sordid history is only a pale reflection. I thought that it was something Plato might have considered but could in no way bring himself to express. I see by your look that you have at last beheld the very incubation of lunacy.

I'm listening. I take it that you have never seen the Archatron.

I would never imagine such a thing to be seeable.

Seeable.

Yes.

As distinct from visible.

I dont know if he's visible or not. I only know that I cant see him. It.

We've had this discussion before. Or something like it.

I know.

The caravan moves on. It's just some sort of sinister archetype.

A troubling notion in clothes.

And an archetype of what.

I dont know. I suppose the catalog of referents goes on at some length.

Who arrived first, the Archatron or the Kid?

The big guy. I think he might even be the reason that the Kid did show up.

Has the Kid ever made any reference to him?

No.

Did you ever talk to your brother about the Archatron?

Yes. I did.

What did he say?

He said he thought straitjackets came in a one-size-fits-all but that he wasnt sure and it could be that there was a small, medium, and large and that he'd have to look it up.

He didnt actually say that.

No. But it worried him. He thought that people hallucinated more than they cared to admit. It didnt necessarily mean that you were nuts. Especially if you were twelve and already nuts by definition. But it worried him anyway and later on he thought that my worldview might be infecting my mathematics. Grothendieck says somewhere that twentieth century mathematics has begun to lose its moral compass. Bobby thought that sort of talk was goofy but when I asked him if he actually knew what Grothendieck meant he had to admit that he didnt. By the time Grothendieck left IHES he was already pretty strange and Bobby thought that he might have had a sort of malign influence on me—which wasnt true—and he also told me that I should rethink submitting my thesis.

He read your thesis.

He read three different drafts of it, actually.

Did he understand it?

Pretty much. He understood what was wrong with it.

And that was?

That nobody could understand it.

You're not serious.

What was wrong with it was that while it proved three problems in topos theory it then set about dismantling the mechanism of the proofs. Not to show that these particular proofs were wrong but that any such proofs ignored their own case. Addressing along the way the more commonly argued claims of mathematical reality.

Mathematics had become a questionable enterprise for you.

I thought about David Bohm. He wrote a really good book on quantum mechanics—largely because Einstein had half convinced him that the theory was faulty. He wanted to get his thoughts down on paper. By the time he'd finished the book he didnt believe in the theory.

Writing your thesis made a skeptic of you.

It didnt help.

Was your brother concerned about your state of mind?

Did he think I was crazy?

All right.

In the vernacular or clinically nuts?

Clinically.

I dont think so. But it could be that the more he thought about it the more concerned he became that maybe I wasnt.

That the news could be worse?

Yes.

Maybe as in what if she is right.

I dont know. Bobby wasnt happy about any of this. I'd stopped talking about it. But by then he'd given up all pretense of an interest in the verity of life on the other side of the glass and he was only interested in how to get rid of it. And by then I wasnt all that sure that I wanted to. Get rid of it.

Why.

Because I knew what my brother did not. That there was an ill-contained horror beneath the surface of the world and there always had been. That at the core of reality lies a deep and eternal demonium. All religions understand this. And it wasnt going away. And that to imagine that the grim eruptions of this century were in any way either singular or exhaustive was simply a folly.

Did you tell your brother that?

Yes. I did.

What did he say?

He leaned and put his hand on my forehead. As if checking for fever.

Is that true?

Yes.

You were not amused.

No, I was amused.

He must have been concerned that you wouldnt get your doctorate.

Yes. He was.

Did you in fact submit it?

No. I hadnt even done all the course work. I think set theory made an outlaw of me. Poincaré said that it was a disease, Hilbert that it was paradise. At least if you include it in Cantor's general body of work at the time. But it was Riemann who was down there doing the actual excavation. More than one mathematician who saw what he was about understood that it was his intention to drive a stake through Euclid's heart.

Why would he want to do that?

Because he didnt like him. He didnt like his wife or his children or his dog.

I suppose this has to do with the axioms.

No. It has to do with reality. You begin with a point which has no dimension and therefore no reality and extend it into a line. Can an extension of nothing eventuate into something? You have to say so. You cant show so.

Did Riemann show so?

If you say so. It's generally assumed that Riemann's triangles' exceeding a sum of one hundred and eighty degrees is an artifact of the curvature of the earth. But the figures are abstractions. They dont live on the earth. Well, they could live in space. And space bends. Yes it does. But Riemann didnt know that.

I'm not sure I see the point.

No pun intended, I'm sure. It's all right. Neither does anyone else. We should sally on.

Where is it? The thesis.

In a landfill somewhere.

Really?

Really.

But you could reproduce it.

I could. I wont.

Was that all right with your brother?

No. He was upset.

Even though he'd said that it was nonsense.

He didnt say it was nonsense. The argument had segued from the formal to the structural and from there it called the discipline itself into question.

I'm not sure that I understand what it was that you were after.

I know. It ultimately descended into such questions as what it was that you were even talking about when you inquired into the nature of shape and form. The final section was called "The Prestige." There was no QED at the end of it.

Is that a mathematical term? Prestige?

No. It's a term for the third part of a magic act. It describes the moment when the woman you've just seen sawn in half steps out and bows to the crowd.

You were comparing your math to a magic act?

Yes.

But surely you dont think that mathematics is magic?

I think that it's magic if you dont understand it. As you learn more about it it becomes less magical. Then as you realize that there is a clear sense in which you will never understand it it becomes magical again. Most people come to terms with their demons. Not all. Jung tells of a case that suggests that aberrant mental states may not be in themselves an illness but rather a protection against a greater one. We know that consciousness never goes to zero except in death. He had a comatose patient at the Burghölzli who came down with a serious illness while still in the coma. Until he finally sat up in bed and began to order the nurses about. This went on until he recovered. Whereupon he went back to sleep. Never to wake again. I dont even know if the story is true. Probably it is. If for no other reason than the story is smarter than Jung. Who after all had to hire someone to take the math exam for medical school. Anyway the answer is yes. I do think that he was sent. Nothing else really computes.

I'm sorry. You've lost me.

The Kid.

Oh. Yes. By whom was he sent then?

I dont know. He's no more mysterious than the deeper questions about any other reality. Or mathematics. For that matter. Forms turning in a nameless void. Salvaged out of a bleak sea of the incomputable. Time's up.

VI

Good morning.

Good morning.

You look different.

The slow pallor. The distant gaze. You yourself look a bit exercised.

I was lucky to get here. The roads are terrible.

You're careful not to tell me much about yourself. Your life. Maybe you should hew less closely to the party line.

Well. I told you that I was married. Twice to the same woman. Two kids. What did you want to know?

What's your daughter's name?

Rachel.

Lovely name. A sad name. How old is she?

She's nine.

What's she like?'

She's not sad.

Not yet.

You dont think that's an odd thing to say?

I think you name your children who you want them to be. What would she be like if her name was Dolly? She's thoughtful.

She is thoughtful. Yes.

Tall and slender. She has dark hair. She's smart. She likes cats. She's hard on her little brother. Unless he hurts himself. Then she's the first one there.

You could do this in the circus sideshow.

Maybe I'll meet her sometime. Has she ever been here?

No. I dont think so. No. She hasnt.

You should go ahead.

As in my turn?

Yes.

Okay. What could you tell me that you've never told anyone before?

Any analyst before.

Okay. Any analyst.

Tons of stuff.

Just something of some significance. That you've thought about. Maybe a question that you've thought about raising but never did.

You think that we're running out of time.

I dont know. Are we?

Dunno.

It doesnt have to be something personal. It doesnt even have to be something about you.

Who would it be about?

It could be anything. It could be a decision that you'd arrived at. Or something that you'd realized.

Realized.

Yes.

Odd locution. Literally of course it means to make real. What if I just told you some monstrous lie?

Why would you?

I wouldnt. I said what if. I think you tend to believe about anything I tell you.

Am I too trusting? Too gullible?

No. I think you're about right.

Go ahead.

I went on the road. A geographical. I spent a couple of months just driving around the country. I ate and showered in truckstops and slept mostly in the car.

Were you doing math?

No. I did a lot of reading. I'd check in to some cheap hotel in Boise or someplace and just hole up. I'd leave the car in a mall parkinglot and take the coil wire with me.

What was the point?

That was the point. I was reading four and five books a day. Some of the stuff I was looking for had been out of print forever. I would bogus up university IDs and get a library card. I read books that hadnt been checked out in forty years.

Where was Bobby at this time?

I dont know. I think he was driving around the country cashing in gold coins.

And the Kid?

He'd show up from time to time. Usually a bit out of sorts. Sometimes I'd wake up in a hotel room somewhere and I would hardly even know how I got there. Lying on the bed in my clothes. And the Kid would be pacing up and back and he'd be saying things like we dont have much dough but I got us in here for now. We need to just lay low. Think things over. I felt like John Dillinger. What things? What are you talking about? You realize that you havent bathed or eaten in several days. You're not sure where your car is. You go downstairs into the street and it's hot. Midmorning. You walk down to the corner and there's a newspaper-stand there and you take a look and it's the Miami Herald. Okay. That's a start. You go back up to the room and the Kid's gone. You crawl into the bed and pull the sheet over you. You dont have to do anything. You've got a few hours yet before checkout. Nobody knocks on the door. Turns out I've paid for a week. In the afternoon I went out and came across my car parked at an expired meter with a ticket stuck in the windshield. I'd just move my car from street to street. Meter to meter. Ticket to ticket. I went into a little mom and pop grocery and bought some tomatoes and cheese and stuff. Some rolls. Went back to my room but the Kid seemed to really be gone. Actually everything was sort of cool. Except for the drunks banging on your door at odd hours. A deskclerk in a hotel in Topeka Kansas asked me point blank if I was a working girl and I told him to take a good look at me and then to ask himself that if I was a hooker what would I be doing in a shithole like this?

What did he say?

He said I see your point.

What did you think was going to happen?

I didnt know what was going to happen. I thought I might wind up here. I parked in the parkinglot here once and slept in the car. But in the morning I drove on.

You didnt have any friends. Anywhere?

No.

You said you had no friends in high school.

I was elected president of my senior class. But I think they just wanted to see what would happen.

What happened?

Nothing. I was getting ready to leave for college. Anyway, I was only fourteen.

Did you ever tell your brother that you were synesthetic?

Yes. He asked me.

He asked you?

Yes.

What made him think to ask you?

Because Bobby is very smart and he knows lots of things. He could see that I was a good candidate. And he knew that synesthetic kids often keep it to themselves because they see that the other kids just think they're weird.

Was he synesthetic?

No. Or slightly. He'd had a couple of episodes but it wasnt a part of his life. Anyway, after that I told him everything.

You told him about the Kid.

Yes. The summer after that he came home and he spent the whole summer at the house and that was the best time. The last best time. I had a fellowship at Chicago for that fall. He came home and we started dating.

You started dating?

I dont know what else you'd call it. We went out every night.

You went out?

He used to take me to these honkytonks on the outskirts of Knoxville. The Indian Rock. The Moonlight Diner. I would dress up like a floozy and dance my ass off. Bobby would play with the band. He'd play breakdowns on the mandolin. I told people that we were married. To keep the fights to a minimum. I loved it. Are you sure you want to hear this?

I think so. Why?

It might get a bit raunchy.

How old were you?

Fourteen. Just.

You told people that you and your brother were married?

They didnt know he was my brother. For the most part.

Was that all right with him?

I suppose. It was meant to be sort of a joke.

Maybe I should ask you if you're sure you want to go on with this.

In for a shilling.

Because I'm guessing that it wasnt a joke for you.

No.

Anything that you'd like to add to that?

Just that I wanted to marry him. As you may have rightly guessed. I always had. It's not very complicated.

You wanted to marry your brother?

I wanted to be married to him. Yes.

I see.

I doubt it. Anyway, the cat's out of the bag.

Did you tell your brother this?

Yes.

You told him that you wanted to marry him.

Yes. I asked him to marry me.

You asked your brother to marry you.

Yes.

You were serious.

Very.

What did he say?

He told me to sober up.

Had you been drinking?

No. I dont drink. It's just an expression.

And you didnt think that there was anything wrong with this?

I thought that the fact that it wasnt acceptable wasnt really our problem. I knew that he loved me. He was just afraid. I'd known this was coming for a long time. There was no place else for me to go. I knew that we would have to run away but I didnt care about any of that. I kissed him in the car. We kissed twice, actually. The first time just very softly. He patted my hand as if in all innocence and turned to start the car but I put my hand on his cheek and turned him to me and we kissed again and this time there was no innocence in it at all and it took his breath. It took mine. I put my face on his shoulder and he said we cant do this. You know we cant do this. I wanted to say that I knew no such thing. I should have. I kissed his cheek. I had no belief in his resolution but I was wrong. We never kissed again.

You're serious about this.

Yes.

You'd decided on all this even before the evening in question.

The evening in question. Yes. I'd known for years. I told him that I was all right with waiting. Then I started crying. I couldnt stop crying.

Did you really think that your brother would marry you?

Yes. I did. He should have.

And you would, what? Live in another country?

Yes.

Didnt you think that you could find someone else?

There wasnt anyone else. There never would be. There wasnt for him either. He just didnt know it yet.

How old were you when you realized that you were in love with your brother?

Probably twelve. Maybe younger. Younger. The hallway.

And you never looked back. As the saying goes.

It's not so easy to explain, but it was pretty clear to me that there was not some alternate view of things to embrace. He was away at school and I only lived for when he would come home. At Christmas or whenever.

And on the night in question you told him everything.

Yes.

Didnt you know what he would say?

I didnt care. We had to make a beginning.

And the fact that he seemed to more or less reject you didnt change anything.

No. I asked him who it was that he thought I should marry but of course he had no answer. He kept saying that I was fourteen but I told him that he was the one who was talking nonsense, not me. What if one of us died? Who has forever?

How old was your brother?

Twenty-one.

Didnt he have girlfriends?

He tried. It never came to anything. I wasnt jealous. I wanted him to see other girls. I wanted him to see the truth of his situation.

That he was in love with you.

Yes. Bone of his bone. Too bad. We were like the last on earth. We could choose to join the beliefs and practices of the millions of dead beneath our feet or we could begin again. Did he really have to think about it? Why should I have no one? Why should he? I told him that I'd no way even to know if there was justice in my heart if I had no one to love and love me. You cannot credit yourself with a truth that has no resonance. Where is the reflection of your worth? And who will speak for you when you are dead?

I'm sorry. I didnt mean to make you cry.

You didnt.

Do you want to stop?

No.

What else?

I told him that I wanted to have his child.

You told your brother that you wanted to have his child.

Look. It's no good you repeating these things to me as if to limn the horror and the lunacy of them. You cant see the world I see. You cant see through these eyes. You never will.

I'm sure that's true.

I told my brother that I was in love with him and that I always had been and that I would be until I died and that it wasnt my fault that he was my brother. You could look at it as just a piece of bad luck. I told him that he should resign.

Resign?

Yes. Resign his brotherhood.

How would he do that?

I dont know. Turn around three times and say I denounce this bond of blood.

And then marry you.

And then marry me. Yes. Although you could say that the facts were a bit more raw than that.

Meaning that you wanted to have sex with your brother?

Meaning.

The stigma of incest had no meaning for you.

What do you want me to say? That I'm a bad girl? Who is Westermarck to me or me to Westermarck? I wanted to do it with my brother. I always did. I still do. There are worse things in the world.

You must have seen that this was something of a torment for him.

I know. I just hoped that he would come to his senses. That he would suddenly come to understand what he'd always known. I suppose I thought to shock him out of his complacency. I would hold his hand. I'd sit close against him driving home and put my head on his shoulder. I suppose I was shameless but then shame was not something I was really concerned with. I knew that I had only one chance and one love. And I wasnt wrong about his feelings. I saw the way he looked at me.

You're so sure.

Yes. At spring break we'd gone to Patagonia Arizona to an inn there and I couldnt sleep and I went to his room and sat on his bed and I thought that he would put his arms around me and kiss me but he didnt. I hadnt known until that night that at its worst lust could be something close to anguish. I thought that something had changed at dinner but it hadnt. I'd become concerned that if I died he would think it his fault and that was a concern that was never to leave me. A friend once told me that those who choose a love that can never be fulfilled will be hounded by a rage that can never be extinguished.

Are you enraged?

I dont know. I know that you can make a good case that all of human sorrow is grounded in injustice. And that sorrow is what is left when rage is expended and found to be impotent.

Why dont we have some tea?

Is it that bad?

Just give me a minute.

Take your time. I'll be looking at your notes.

———

Are you okay?

Yes.

All right. The fact that you own nothing.

Yes.

Might divesting yourself of everything be a way of preparing for death?

I dont think there is some way to prepare for death. You have to make one up. There's no evolutionary advantage to being good at dying. Who would you leave it to? The thing you are dealing with— time—is immalleable. Except that the more you harbor it the less of it you have. The liquor of being is leaking out onto the ground. You need to hurry. But the haste itself is consuming what you wish to preserve. You cant deal with what it is you've been sent to deal with. It's too hard.

I dont disagree. I think. Even if I probably couldnt say it quite so elaborately. Or wouldnt.

Elaborately. Is that code for hysterical?

No. I take it you wouldnt characterize your brother's racing motorcars as a death wish.

No. I'm not a fan of nonsense.

You said that a number of physicists have taken up mountain climbing.

Yes. But it wouldnt have worked for him.

Why is that?

Because he wasnt afraid of heights. There'd be no purpose in it.

What was he afraid of?

Depths.

Was he afraid of driving fast?

I never met a racecar driver who was afraid of driving fast. They all think that wrecks are for other people. There's an old saw in racing to the effect that it's not going fast that kills you it's stopping fast. No one talks about it but it's always there. There's a photograph of Nina Rindt taken at Monza two years ago. She's beautifully dressed and she is sitting looking out across the racecourse. Her husband has just been killed but she doesnt know it yet. Bobby and I were at their house in Geneva. There was a Formula Two racecar hanging nosedown from the livingroom wall. She'd been a model and she was very beautiful. She came from a wealthy Finnish family. They were very much in love, she and Jochen, and I was very jealous. Fool me. I didnt know that we were to be sisters in the only way that mattered.

You said you were shameless where Bobby was concerned. How shameless?

How much prurience are you up for?

I dont know. I dont know how prurient it gets.

I told him about a dream I had.

A dream.

Yes.

Of intimacy.

Yes.

What was his reaction?

About what you would expect.

He was horrified.

He had cause. I suppose.

It was particularly graphic.

It was pretty graphic.

Did you frequently have such dreams about your brother?

No. Mostly I dreamt about us being together. Living together. I dreamt about us being married. Not so much now. Not so much. Do you find that sad? I suppose not.

I dont know what I find that.

We were at a cabin in the woods. Maybe sort of like the cabin that my father lived in but it was on a lake. I think that it might have been here in Wisconsin. It was in the fall of the year and there was a fire in the fireplace and there may have been snow on the ground. I'm not sure. It was a big stone fireplace and you could see the flickering of the fire from the bedroom and there were candles everywhere.

When was this?

Two years ago. Do you want me to tell you or not?

Yes.

There were candles everywhere and we were naked and he looked up at me from between my legs and smiled and his face in the candlelight was all shiny with girljuice and then I woke up. My orgasm woke me up.

You told your brother this?

Yes.

What did he say?

He said. He said you cant talk to me like that. You mustnt ever talk to me like that again.

And?

And what?

What did you say?

I said that I wouldnt. And I didnt.

What were your feelings about this?

About the dream?

Yes.

Regret.

You were sorry that you told him?

No. I was sorry it was a dream. That's all. I'm tired.

All right. Will I see you on Wednesday?

I dont know. Yes. You will see me.

VII

How are you doing?

I'm okay.

I havent seen that sweater before.

It's a loaner.

You dont have a coat, do you?

I'm not going anywhere.

I could bring you one.

Okay. What about galoshes?

Why not. What happened to your hair?

Leonard whacked some of it off.

What did he use to cut it?

Is it that bad?

I only wondered where he got the scissors.

Not telling.

Okay. I replayed our last session.

How was that.

It occurred to me that when a patient unburdens herself of some intimacy—even if the therapist might like to think that he's earned a new level of trust, it may not be that at all.

So what may it be at all? Do you think.

It could be that she's afraid that the therapy is threatening to reveal some other intimacy she considers more private. Although I grant you that might be hard to imagine.

I would tell you something I dont want you to know in order to conceal something that I really dont want you to know.

Something like that.

Sounds a bit shrinky to me.

I know. Actually it sounds like something I once said.

Anyway, having uncovered this deviousness in your patient, what horrors do you think she might be concealing?

I dont know. What have you got?

Marlon Brando in *The Wild One.*

I'm sorry?

That was his line. Anyway, why would I tell you? Isnt that the point of the maneuver?

Do you still imagine an intimate relationship with your brother?

My brother's dead.

I'm sorry. Was this why you left IHES? Well. Yes. Of course. I suppose. I guess what I wanted to ask is if you intend to return.

No.

Where did you learn German?

In Germany.

You speak it without an accent.

How would you know?

To my ear at least. My grandmother spoke German. German and Yiddish.

There was a German driver who was interested in me.

Were you having an affair with him?

No. But Bobby didnt know that. I told him it was none of his business. I just wanted him to see what a fake he was.

He was jealous.

Tell me about it.

Did you like Germany?

Yes. It surprised me. I think I worked harder at German than at any other language. I had about ten colorcoded notebooks. The articles are tricky. And it's a very mannered society. I kept a log in my say and do book.

Your friend had left the Institute by then. Is that correct?

Yes.

But that's not why you decided to give up mathematics.

No. I would have anyway.

Do you miss it?

It's like missing the dead. They're not coming back. Old foundational issues will probably continue to trouble my dreams. And there are times when I miss the world of calculation itself. Solving problems. When things suddenly fall into place after days of labor it's like a lost animal coming in out of the rain. Your thought is to say there you are. To say I was so worried. You hardly even bother to review your work. You just know. That what you are looking at is true. It's a joyful thing.

Have you ever cut yourself?

Have I ever cut myself.

Yes.

You really take the plaid rabbit. Did you know that?

No. Your fantasies about suicide. Where are we with this?

I wouldnt tell you if I knew.

What is it that you feel guilty about?

Other than being born I suppose.

Other. Yes.

I think I'd have to say first of all that I seriously doubt that people are driven to suicide by guilt. When were we ever so virtuous?

When you said goodbye to the Kid.

Yes.

He wanted to know if you would miss him.

Yes.

What did you say?

I didnt know what to say. I was suffocating in sadness. It was not something I'd expected.

But you wont see him again.

No.

I dont want to ask how you could be so sure. After how many years?

Eight. The Ogdoad.

The Ogdoad?

In Gnostic years.

You have no clear sense of what it is that he represented.

He represented himself. He is his own being, not mine. That's really all I learned. However you choose to construe such a statement. I never met a counselor who didnt want to kill him.

At the end you were actually fond of him.

He is small and frail and brave. What is the inner life of an eidolon? Do his thoughts and his questions originate with him? Do mine with me? Is he my creature? Am I his? I saw how he made do with his paddles and that he was ashamed for me to see. His turn of speech, his endless pacing. Was that my work? I've no such talent. I cant answer your questions. The tradition of trolls or demons standing sentinel against inquiry must be as old as language. Still, maybe a friend must be someone you can touch. I dont know. I no longer have an opinion about reality. I used to. Now I dont. The first rule of the world is that everything vanishes forever. To the extent that you refuse to accept that then you are living in a fantasy.

Have you ever been in ICP? There's no record of it.

No. But that's probably where I'm headed. Together with my big mouth.

It's just that I'm responsible for you. It wouldnt really change anything. It might give me a better chance to see what's going on with you.

I'd like to have at least some privacy. Your minder follows you around everywhere. They watch you shower. You cant wear anything on your feet. I'm sure I would draw Miss Surlynurse.

Let me think about it.

What if I went back on the meds.

Would you?

No.

We could go over a few of them.

You dont even have a diagnosis but you're ready to prescribe.

So why did you bring it up?

I just wanted to see if you'd trot out your pharmaceuticals. Lithium of course always comes last because it's not patentable. You cant turn a buck with a thing like that. Otherwise the names themselves are pretty wonderful. Depakote, Seroquel. Risperdal. Jesus. Who makes this shit up?

You believe all this is a pharmaceutical conspiracy.

No. I really dont. Why am I on your ass? Dreams are frail. If you can drug them into being no reason why you shouldnt be able to drug them out again.

Is this the side of you that counselors have described as difficult?

I suppose you could ask them what they expected of a mental patient. Anyway, in the end I was hardly even a patient. But they were still difficult doctors.

You studied the literature the better to confound them.

I didnt study anything. What was there to study? If they could be confounded by their own doctrines wouldnt they have been already?

You spoke of waking from ugly dreams. Did you ever see anything that was truly troubling?

I never saw monsters. Creatures going around carrying their heads. I always sensed that the worst of it transcended representation. You couldnt put together something for them to look like. You didnt have the parts.

Is this something that is always there?

No. And sometimes everything would just go away. It still does. Sometimes in the winter in the dark I'd wake and everything that smacked of dread would have lifted up and stolen away in the night and I would just be lying there with the snow blowing against the glass. I'd think that maybe I should turn on the lamp but then I'd just lie there and listen to the quiet. The wind in the quiet. There are times now when I see those patients in their soiled nightshirts lying on gurneys in the hallway with their faces to the wall that I ask myself what humanity means. I would ask does it include me.

Did you want to be included?

I did want to be included. I just wasnt willing to pay the entry fee. On my better days I could even grant that we were the same creatures. Much was the same and little different. The same unlikely forms. Elbows. Skulls. The remnants of a soul.

I'm surprised to hear those sentiments.

Mental illness doesnt seem to occur in animals. Why do you think that is?

I dont know. But I imagine you have some notion about it.

Why do you imagine that?

Because you raised the question. You're like a lawyer.

As in dont ask a question you dont know the answer to.

Yes. Anyway, what about dogs with rabies?

Rabies is not a mental illness. It's a disease of the brain.

Interesting distinction. All right, why? They're not smart enough?

I dont think that's it. Cetaceans are pretty smart and they dont appear to be afflicted with lunacy. I think you have to have language to have craziness.

I guess so you can hear the voices in your head.

Not sure why. But you have to understand what the advent of language was like. The brain had done pretty well without it for quite a few million years. The arrival of language was like the invasion of a parasitic system. Co-opting those areas of the brain that were the least dedicated. The most susceptible to appropriation.

A parasitic invasion.

Yes.

You're serious.

Yes. The inner guidance of a living system is as necessary to its survival as oxygen and hydrogen. The governance of any system evolves coevally with the system itself. Everything from a blink to a cough to a decision to run for your life. Every faculty but language has the same history. The only rules of evolution that language follows are those necessary to its own construction. A process that took little more than an eyeblink. The extraordinary usefulness of language turned it into an overnight epidemic. It seems to have spread to every remote pocket of humanity almost instantly. The same isolation of groups that led to their uniqueness would seem to have been no protection at all against this invasion and both the form of language and the strategies by which it gained purchase in the brain seem all but universal. The most immediate requirement was for an increased capacity for making sounds. Language seems to have originated in South Africa and this requirement probably accounts for the clicks in the Khoisan languages. The fact that there were more things to name than sounds to name them with. In any case the physical facility for speech was probably the most difficult hurdle. The pharynx became elongated until the apparatus in its present form has all but strangled its owner. We're the only mammalian species that cant swallow and articulate at the same time. Think of a cat growling while it eats and then try it yourself. Anyway, the unconscious system of guidance is millions of years old, speech less than a hundred thousand. The brain had no idea any of this was coming. The unconscious must have had to do all sorts of scrambling around to accommodate a system that proved perfectly relentless. Not only is it comparable to a parasitic invasion, it's not comparable to anything else.

That's quite a dissertation.

What makes it interesting is that language evolved from no known need. It was just an idea. Lysenko rising from the dead. And the idea, again, was that one thing could represent another. A biological system under successful assault by human reason.

I'm not sure I've heard evolutionary biology discussed in such warlike terms. And the unconscious doesnt like to speak to us because of its million year history devoid of language?

Yes. It solves problems and is perfectly capable of telling us the answers. But million year old habits die hard. It could easily say: Kekulé, it's a fucking ring. But it feels more comfortable cobbling up a hoop snake and rolling it around inside Kekulé's skull while he's dozing in front of the fire. It's why your dreams are filled with drama and metaphor.

I dont know what the hoop snake refers to.

It refers to the configuration of the benzene molecule. It's not important.

Troubling words. But I think you've suggested that the advent of language, aside from the enormous value of it, was disruptive.

Very disruptive. Of a piece with its value. Creative destruction. All sorts of talents and skills must have been lost. Mostly communicative. But also things like navigation and probably even the richness of dreams. In the end this strange new code must have replaced at least part of the world with what can be said about it. Reality with opinion. Narrative with commentary.

And sanity with madness, dont forget.

Yes. I wont.

And the arrival of universal war.

And the arrival.

How did we get on this subject?

It's all right. We can drop it.

What else?

What else what?

How long has synesthesia been around? Is there something linguistic about that?

Not that I'm aware. It seems pretty primeval. Color, taste, smell. Although I'm not sure that conflating the senses is all that good an idea. Survivalwise.

Autism? More specifically of the idiot savant variety.

Linguistic to the bone.

To the bone.

Synesthesia might be ours as well. Now that I think about it. A synesthetic who sees the number five as red in arabic might very well see it red in roman as well. Which suggests that what they see as red is a concept and not the physical number. Whatcha think?

And this was something that you kept from the other kids.

Among other things. Quite a few other things, in fact. It helps you to remember.

What helps you to remember?

Synesthesia. It's easier to remember two things than one. It's why it's easier to remember the words of a song than the words of a poem. For instance. The music is an armature upon which you assemble the words.

What else?

Lots else.

The other kids thought you were weird.

It wasnt a supposition.

You agreed with them.

I could see it from where they stood.

Were any of them good at math?

No.

Not even a little bit?

Not even.

Was Bobby?

I think you asked me that. He was good at math. Just not good enough. He changed his major to physics. I didnt tell him that I thought he should. He just did it. He was good at doing numbers in his head. Better than me. Some people think that's math. Can I ask you something?

Of course.

Do I smell?

Why? Have you been neglecting yourself?

That bad, huh?

You cant shower with someone watching?

I shower.

It's fairly common on the ward. People tend to neglect things like hygiene.

What else is like hygiene?

I dont know. Has someone been critical of your appearance?

Not that I know of. I know sometimes I look like I left the house in a hurry. I used to enjoy getting dressed up to go dancing. But that was costume.

Make-believe.

Yes.

You would get dressed up for Bobby.

I suppose. Yes.

I'm sorry.

It's all right. There were times I'd see him looking at me and I would leave the room crying. I knew that I'd never be loved like that again. I just thought that we would always be together. I know you think I should have seen that as more aberrant than I did, but my life is not like yours. My hour. My day. I used to dream about our first time together. I do yet. I wanted to be revered. I wanted to be entered like a cathedral.

Maybe we should talk about something else.

I know.

You've snarled a bit at Jung but I dont think we've said much about Freud.

We were jung and easily freudened.

What is that?

Nothing. A line from Joyce. I think the case histories are interesting. Of course there's always something for sale. The dream book is good to the extent that it's not a novel. I think he has a shaky view of our inner life. Maybe moreso even than Jung. It's not that complicated. If they'd thought a bit more about biological evolution and spent less time cooking up nutty theories they might have uncovered a few simple truths.

You wouldnt agree that their theories are nevertheless based upon actual observation?

Like astrology.

You're not serious.

Maybe not. At least Freud doesnt attempt to say what dreams are.

And that's a good thing.

Yes. Because he doesnt know. Creating a language for nonexistent categories is not a particularly good strategy for those wishing to leave some sort of intellectual legacy. There has to be a metaphor for such enterprises. Some image of theoretical bones whitening in the waste.

Mathematics is subject to no such weathering.

No. When mathematics is gone it will all be gone.

But still . . .

But still. And yet. Life is hard. I will always love mathematics but I'm a granitehearted skeptic and it may be that my doubts cannot be addressed by logical inquiry. The whereof that one cannot.

Is there a single insight that supports most of modern mathematics?

Oh this is good.

Sorry.

No. It's not a lame question. It's just that we dont know the answer. Things like the deeps of cohomology or Cantor's discontinuum are tainted with the flavor of unguessed worlds. We can see the footprints of algebras whose entire domain is immune to commutation. Matrices whose hatchings cast a shadow upon the floor of their origins and leave there an imprint to which they no longer conform. Homological algebra has come to shape a good deal of modern mathematics. But in the end the world of computation will simply absorb it.

Gödel's work I take it will never suffer the fate of Freud's. The bones of it bleaching on the ground or whatever.

My railings against the platonists are a thing of the past. Assuming at last that one could, what would be the advantage of ignoring the transcendent nature of mathematical truths. There is nothing else that all men are compelled to agree upon, and when the last light in the last eye fades to black and takes all speculation with it forever I think it could even be that these truths will glow for just a moment in the final light. Before the dark and the cold claim everything.

Did you want to take a break?

I guess. If you like.

Did you want a cigarette?

No. I'm all right.

It's not understood, is it? What mathematics is.

No.

Will it ever be?

No.

Your friend Gödel was really a hard line platonist.

Yes. He thought that mathematical objects had the same reality as trees and stones.

That seems an odd view.

It is an odd view. I suppose other mathematicians tend to take Gödel's views at face value, but those views could reflect a skepticism concerning reality itself. As for myself I've never seen a six. I dont know what could possibly constitute a mathematical object. In my experience everything mathematical is in the form of a directive. The numerical concept of six is totally inert. Gödel wasnt always a platonist, but he's not the first scientist to accept an implausible theory simply because it explained the facts. After the 1931 papers it was clear to him that we are capable of mathematical insights that a Universal Truth Machine is not. But why Gödel could see no problem with the notion of mathematical abstractions as factual entities I couldnt tell you. Platonists seem more or less silent as to the origin of mathematics and remarkably unconcerned as to what might be the purpose of computation in an uninhabited universe. I think spookthink is a lot more common among mathematicians than is generally supposed. In the end Gödel became something akin to a Deist. Not that he pursued any sort of spiritual practice. It's a tradition that runs from Pythagoras to Newton to Cantor. Who after all attributed a supernatural origin to the transfinites. Aleph Zero. Aleph One. It couldnt have helped his cause. His notions of relative infinities had to await the death of an entire generation of German mathematicians before these notions could even get a hearing. Is the Universe intelligent? Isnt that what's at stake? My brother used to say not very. Perhaps sufficient unto the day. Gödel never says outright that there is a covenant to which all of mathematics subscribes but you get a clear sense that the hope is there. I know the allure. Some shimmering palimpsest of eternal abidement. But to claim that numbers somehow exist in the Universe with no intelligence to enable them does not require a different sort of mathematics. It requires a different sort of universe.

Is there such a universe?

Gödel has notions that are simply bizarre. The circularity of time works mathematically but it will never deal with meeting your dead grandfather. His notions about God. I just put his platonism in the same box. But it wouldnt stay there. Rather slowly it sank in that this is Gödel we're talking about and while he could have goofy notions about all sorts of things could he really have goofy notions about mathematics?

And what did you conclude?

I'm still concluding.

Which way are you leaning?

I've gone back and re-read the 1931 papers twice. The last time I re-read them I dreamt about them. I dreamt about the second paper. And I woke up and as I woke up the dream began to dissolve. The dream and the story of the dream. And I knew that in the dream was an understanding that was simply a gift and it was receding in the darkness and I sat up in bed and called out after it but it simply fell to pieces in my mind and after that I saw the insights of the paper in a very different way but I dont know if the dream is any part of that understanding and I suspect I never will.

Were there numbers in the dream?

Of course that's the question, isnt it? No there were not. The dream consisted entirely of understanding.

I'm not sure I understand that. But it was never coming back.

It was never coming back.

Your view of things changed.

Yes. I began to have doubts about my heretofore material view of the universe.

Was this something that came about slowly?

I dont know. I dont know what slowly is. Gödel talks about several mathematicians who had transformative experiences. I suppose I should look them up. He never had such an experience. I think he might have been jealous. I think the dream is still there. I think it knows whether or not it should revisit me. Or me it. Gödel likes to complain about people not understanding his Indeterminacy papers. I re-read them and I saw that he was probably right. I hadnt understood them.

Do you understand them now?

Define understand.

All right. Moving on. You think that math is done by the unconscious.

Yes. I dont know any math. I just try to get it written down when it shows up.

I think that must be something of an exaggeration.

Maybe. Something. Why is this interesting to you?

Because it is to you. How long ago was the dream?

The night before last.

No it wasnt.

Six months ago. Maybe seven.

If the dream . . . What was the word? Revisited you? If you could remember the dream would you tell me?

I dont know. I'd have to take a look at it. What if it was obscene?

Obscene mathematics.

Sure. Why not?

So what was it that you understood?

Vis-à-vis Gödel?

Vis-à-vis.

I think I saw what he saw. That finding the limits of a system was not just finding the limits. It was finding what lay beyond the limits. You just had to find the limits first.

And what lay beyond the limits?

In this case it was the realization that what you had long suspected was in fact true. That mathematics had no limits. That it was inexhaustible. There was no longer any question about that. And now you had to sit down and think about the universe.

And what did you think? About the universe.

You thought that your inquiry was going to labor under a shrinking availability of the empirical. Even while you worked the universe was receding.

So what would you bring to bear on the inquiry?

I suppose the only thing that you had. Your mind.

And why would you think that your mind was up to the task?

Because we're here. We're not someplace else. And there is nothing else to know. Some of Gödel's notions were beyond questionable. I thought about his platonism but then I thought that it was not so different from Frege's. Take another look? Not much help. I thought that perhaps the same daring that had led them to their foundational ideas might very well produce other inquiries indistinguishable from gibberish. I put all that away for a while. But it wouldnt stay away. I disagreed more and more with Aristotle. He came to seem more like this blank slate guy. I knew that it was just not so that at birth we were not human beings. I get it that he understood that the mind has a form but he didnt seem to understand what that meant. The mind has to be capable of its own existence.

I dont understand what that means.

I know. I just dont know some other way to put it. I understood that if you allowed yourself to become totally entangled you might not find your way out again. Worse, you might not want to.

Yes.

Abidement. Is that a word?

No. The noun would be abidance. But abidance is a general state to abidement's specific. There is no answer to the question of unanimity among mathematicians. My new friend Chihara—perhaps a fan of Gödel but certainly not of his intuitions—says that mathematicians regarded as biological organisms are basically quite similar.

Is this how he explains their agreement about mathematics? By saying that they are all alike?

I think that most mathematicians would miss the humor in that statement. And it would hardly explain our disagreement about almost everything else. I suppose too that you could say that mathematical intuition only explains an access to mathematics and not to its existence.

So how do you explain its existence?

Maybe the best you can do is point at it. After Wittgenstein.

It's the problems that constitute the body of mathematics, not the answers. Which the problems assume.

Is that true?

I dont know what's true. But maybe that would account for the sense of discovery.

Are we circling the notion of tautology in mathematics?

Rather nice that. Circling the tautology.

But you're still an admirer of Gödel.

Very much.

And your new friend?

Chihara.

Yes. Would he be an admirer also?

I think so. I think a success in science at an early age carries unsuspected burdens. And the greatest of these is fear. Chihara would know about that.

Fear? Of what?

Of being wrong. When Dirac was asked recently why he didnt just come out and announce that the particle lurking in his calculations was an anti-electron what do you think he said?

I dont know.

Pure cowardice.

What else?

Re Gödel?

Yes. He seems to take up a lot of space.

The 1931 papers were motivated by Gödel's reading of Russell and Whitehead's *Principia*. Russell believed that Gödel was the only person to have read it in its entirety and he was amazed at Gödel's grasp of it. Of course it was never finished. Russell saw the problem with it and he begged Whitehead not to publish it. They seldom spoke afterwards. A situation not helped by Russell's continually trying to fuck Whitehead's young wife. Russell had a limited social life at the time and he said that if you couldnt fuck your friends' wives then who were you supposed to fuck?

He didnt say that.

No. Or not to my knowledge. I think it was more just an unspoken principle with him. Whitehead tried to finish the fourth volume on his own but in the end he had to give it up. I think working with Russell all those years had given him a false evaluation of the difficulty of the project.

Russell was a really good mathematician.

Yes.

But he gave it up. Mathematics.

Yes.

Because of Wittgenstein?

Most people—Russell included—say that it was because of Wittgenstein. But the real reason is that Russell wanted to be famous. And he knew that mathematics couldnt do that for him. And of course he was right. And he did become famous. He was recognized the world over and he had endless women. Not all of them the wives of friends.

Did he give up philosophy?

Essentially. He took to writing popular books. I think he came to see attempting to understand the universe as a fool's errand.

A universe containing neither light nor dark.

Nor certitude nor peace nor help for pain.

Something about a darkling plain.

Yes.

Why are people not more interested in science?

They're afraid of it. Even educated people often prefer craziness. Aliens, Velikovsky. Flying saucers.

Craziness.

Yes.

Well. So much for Gödel?

Gödel is forever.

Do you believe that?

No.

All right. Can you juggle?

Well, you did it.

I did what?

You finally surprised me. Can I juggle?

Yes.

Yes. The basics. Three tennisballs. Why?

I just thought it was something you would try. What else can you do?

I dont know. Such as what?

Anything.

I can read backwards. I can read something in a mirror. Who is that? Leonardo? I can write a paper so that the margins are justified. Not the contents necessarily. I dont think Leonardo could do that. Even if he had a typewriter.

I dont understand.

If I'm typing I can make each line come out the same length as the one before. As if it were printed.

I dont see how you could do that. I wouldnt think that would be possible.

You just substitute whatever words are needed in order for the lines to come out the right length.

While you're typing.

While you're typing. Yes.

You dont have to stop and puzzle it out.

No. You just do it.

I'll have to take your word for it.

It's just a trick. I wouldnt try it. It's almost as hard to break as it is to learn.

You still dont have periods anymore.

Jesus.

Jesus?

It's just the things that you guys get up to. I suppose that's in my file.

It's in your medical record, yes.

Nosey parkers.

You use a lot of English expressions. Did you live in England?

No.

Do you exercise a lot?

I used to like to go for walks.

You're very thin.

I know. I dont like to eat.

The question came up in conversation with a colleague as to whether excessive mental exertion might not have some of the same effects as the physical.

As regards menses.

Yes.

Interesting. Supposedly you dont menstruate above fourteen thousand feet either.

Is that true?

I dont know. So I read. We've got thirteen minutes. Do you think we could have some tea?

Of course. Give me a minute.

———

English breakfast tea.

You sound dubious.

It's all right.

All we have is the powdered creamer.

It's okay.

Do you see very much of your friend Leonard?

We chat. He told me you looked him up.

I did.

What did you find out?

About you I suppose.

I dont care. I talk to him because he's funny. And he's bright. He's on Navane.

I dont know what medications he's taking.

He's a Navanite. We tend to laugh at the same things. Even if sometimes not for the same reason.

Do you find him stable?

Stable for Leonard.

Why was he committed? Originally.

He burned down the family house and ran away. When they found him in the woods he couldnt think of anything to say so he just started speaking gibberish.

You dont think there's anything wrong with him.

I think there's plenty wrong with him.

He eloped about a year ago. I think he was gone for three days.

Yes. Well. He understands that if you try to escape from the crazyhouse then you must not be crazy. Apparently he created something of a row in group last week. Well. Maybe not a row.

About what?

He kept complaining about everything until they finally turned on him and asked him just what it was that he wanted. That seemed to stop him and he gave it some thought and finally he said that he just wanted to be happy. At which they turned on him all over again and said no no no, Leonard. Realistic goals.

Is he suicidal?

Leonard?

Yes.

Of course. Well. I shouldnt have said that. Sometimes I forget you're on the other side.

The other side?

Yes.

Okay. Where were we?

I think the subject was my monthlies. Their whereabouts.

Do you think about sex?

Yes. Dont you?

Well. I have a certain history where the subject is concerned. But then I sometimes forget that I'm talking to someone for whom the imaginary has a special place. Did Romania become less appealing as it became more real?

I dont know. Probably. It's certainly possible that the imaginary is best. Like a painting of some idyllic landscape. The place you would most like to be. That you never will.

I'm not sure what you're saying.

I'm not either.

That's not like you.

I know.

Are you talking about death?

No. Just about the problem of accessing the world you most wish for.

Would you like some more hot water?

No. Thank you. I think it was just could that be you?

In the picture?

Yes.

You mean how could it be you? Or how could you make it you?

Be you. Let's say.

Like the axemurderer in the mirror?

I dont know. Maybe. Maybe like the expression of a gesture the meaning of which is uncertain. But which in expanding into the world erases a thousand other histories.

You've lost me.

It's all right. When I left Italy I thought that I would go to Romania. But I didnt. I didnt want to be buried in Wartburg. Mostly I didnt want anyone to know about it.

That you'd died.

Yes.

But you didnt.

Die.

No. Go to Romania.

No. I didnt.

All right. How serious was this plan?

Pretty serious. It was called Plan 2-A.

Why was it called Plan 2-A?

It just was. It was subtitled or not 2-B.

The trip was not?

I was not. I thought that I would go to Romania and that when I got there I would go to some small town and buy secondhand clothes in the market. Shoes. A blanket. I'd burn everything I owned. My passport. Maybe I'd just put my clothes in the trash. Change money in the street. Then I'd hike into the mountains. Stay off the road. Take no chances. Crossing the ancestral lands by foot. Maybe by night. There are bears and wolves up there. I looked it up. You could have a small fire at night. Maybe find a cave. A mountain stream. I'd have a canteen for water for when the time came that I was too weak to move about. After a while the water would taste extraordinary. It would taste like music. I'd wrap myself in the blanket at night against the cold and watch the bones take shape beneath my skin and I would pray that I might see the truth of the world before I died. Sometimes at night the animals would come to the edge of the fire and move about and their shadows would move among the trees and I would understand that when the last fire was ashes they would come and carry me away and I would be their eucharist. And that would be my life. And I would be happy.

I think our time is up.

I know. Hold my hand.

Hold your hand?

Yes. I want you to.

All right. Why?

Because that's what people do when they're waiting for the end of something.

A NOTE ON THE TYPE

This book was set in Bodoni, a typeface named after Giambattista Bodoni (1740–1813), the celebrated printer and type designer of Parma. The Bodoni types of today were designed not as faithful reproductions of any one of the Bodoni fonts but rather as a composite, modern version of the Bodoni manner. Bodoni's innovations in type style included a greater degree of contrast in the thick and thin elements of the letters and a sharper and more angular finish of details.

Composed by North Market Street Graphics,
Lancaster, Pennsylvania

Printed and bound by Friesens,
Altona, Manitoba

Designed by Cassandra J. Pappas